This book should be returned to any branch of the
Lancashire County Library on or before the date shown

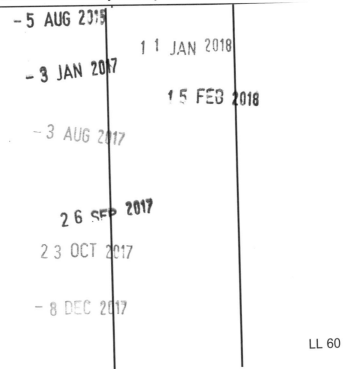

- 5 AUG 2015

1 1 JAN 2018

- 3 JAN 2017

1 5 FEB 2018

- 3 AUG 2017

2 6 SEP 2017

2 3 OCT 2017

- 8 DEC 2017

LL 60

Preston PR1 2UX

# GUNS AT GENESIS

# GUNS AT GENESIS

## WAYNE C. LEE

**WHEELER**
**CHIVERS**

This Large Print edition is published by Wheeler Publishing, Waterville, Maine, USA and by BBC Audiobooks Ltd, Bath, England.
Wheeler Publishing, a part of Gale, Cengage Learning.

**LIBRARY OF CONGRESS CATALOGING-IN-PUBLICATION DATA**

Lee, Wayne C.
  Guns at genesis / by Wayne C. Lee.
    p. cm. — (Wheeler Publishing large print western.)
  ISBN-13: 978-1-4104-2100-5 (pbk. : alk. paper)
  ISBN-10: 1-4104-2100-7 (pbk. : alk. paper)
  I. Title.
PS3523.E34457G8 2009
813'.54—dc22                                           2009029882

BRITISH LIBRARY CATALOGUING-IN-PUBLICATION DATA AVAILABLE

Published in 2009 in the U.S. by arrangement with Golden West Literary Agency.
Published in 2010 in the U.K. by arrangement with Golden West Literary Agency.

U.K. Hardcover: 978 1 408 45802 0 (Chivers Large Print)
U.K. Softcover: 978 1 408 45803 7 (Camden Large Print)

114337342

Printed in the United States of America
1 2 3 4 5 6 7 13 12 11 10 09

# GUNS AT GENESIS

# 1

The minute Sam Trego came in sight of the farm, he was chilled by the feeling that something was wrong. His uncle, Luther Holcomb, should have been in the field at this time of day. He wasn't. Even the house appeared quiet.

Nudging his horse into an easy trot, he let his eyes roam, looking for some tangible evidence to support his uneasy feeling. At the hitchrack, he stepped down, his six-foot-five-inch frame towering over the horse as he surveyed the yard again before concentrating on the house.

Lifting a huge hand, calloused from carrying iron rails, he rubbed a two-day stubble on his chin. His dark eyes, squinting from his sun-browned face, turned flint hard, cautious, defensive, like an uncertain cougar, ready either to attack or run.

With his boots crunching on the gravel, he walked up the path to the house. Lifting his hat, he ran a hand through his unruly brown hair. Aunt Ruth would probably ask him if he'd ever seen a comb. She seldom missed the opportunity.

He started across the porch, raising a fist to knock, when the door burst open and a short woman with graying hair rushed out. Trego had often thought that his Aunt Ruth would have been a tall woman if so much of her hadn't been pushed out into the shape of an overfed Santa Claus.

"Sam!" she shrieked. "Oh, Sam, you're the answer to my prayer!" She charged across the porch, trying to wrap her chubby arms around him.

Trego reached down to catch her in his arms. "I know I've been the object of many prayers but this is the first time I've ever heard that I'm the answer to one." He pushed her back where he could see her tear-stained face. Those stains were not all fresh. "What's wrong, Aunt Ruth?" he asked.

She backed into the house and dropped on a chair. Trego followed and sat down across the table from her.

"Luther's gone." Her voice was almost a whisper now. "Been gone for nearly two weeks."

Trego leaned his two hundred and thirty

pounds forward, making the chair creak. "Gone where?"

"I'm not sure, Sam." She was almost in tears. "He wouldn't tell me where he was going or why. You know that's not like Luther. He did say something about Pace. I think maybe he went to see him. He said he'd be back in a few days but he hasn't come."

That uneasy feeling Trego had experienced when he first saw the empty field was gnawing harder at him now. Ruth Holcomb was his father's sister and her husband, Luther, was as solid as the rocks out along Sage Creek. He wouldn't just go off without telling his wife where he was going or why, not unless there was something terribly wrong.

"Are Pace and Katie having trouble over at Genesis?" Trego asked.

"Not that I know about. Luther came home from town one day all worked up and said he had to be gone a few days. Even if he went to see Pace, he should have been back in less than a week."

Trego got to his feet, feeling the knot growing in his middle. When he had come to Sage Creek, he had sworn he would stay out of trouble. But he could feel himself being pulled into it like a straw sucked into a tornado. He turned to Ruth. "Have you had

9

anybody looking for him?"

"Everybody. Nobody has seen any sign of him. The sheriff even hinted that a lot of men run off and leave their wives. The ninny! As if Luther would do that!"

"A man leaving home for good would take his money. Uncle Luther didn't take his money out of the bank, did he?"

Ruth looked shocked. "I didn't ask. But you know he wouldn't."

Trego nodded, pacing to the window. He doubted if Luther ever had more than one or two thousand dollars of his own in his life. But he did have five thousand dollars of Trego's money right now. For anybody but Luther, that would have been a temptation. Trego and his uncle were going to buy a ranch with their combined money someday. That had been in Trego's mind when he came here.

"I'm going to town, Aunt Ruth," he said. "I probably won't be back till I find Uncle Luther." He headed for the door.

Ruth heaved herself out of the chair. "Not till you've had something to eat! You can look better on a full stomach."

A touch of a smile parted his lips. That sounded more like his Aunt Ruth than anything she'd said since he came. Nobody did anything well unless he was fed, the way she saw it.

"You didn't tell me why you came back here," Ruth said as she banged a pan and a skillet together, shoving them back on the stove so she could stuff more fuel into the firebox.

Trego paced back to the window, a frown tugging at his craggy face. "I've been laying track for the Denver and Rio Grande out in the mountains," he said, turning to face Ruth. "Had an argument with a man in the crew. He kept pushing till it ended in a fight and I killed him." He held up his big hands, staring at them. "With my bare hands, I killed him!"

Ruth turned from the stove. "Is that why you're here? Are you running?"

Trego shook his head. "They called it self defense. He did start the fight. I'd hurt men before in a fight and actually felt good about it. But this was the first time I'd killed, and it made me sick. I knew if I stayed there, I'd probably kill again. I've got the education to be a preacher, you know. Pa saw to that. For the first time since I finished school, the idea sounded good to me."

Ruth stared at him. "You mean you want to be a preacher?"

"I'd rather put men on the right path than in their graves."

11

Ruth shook her head in wonder and flipped the meat in the skillet. "They say you can't really sympathize with a widow until you've lost your own man. Maybe you can sympathize with the sinners now that you've seen both sides of the elephant."

Trego wasn't sure. He just knew that he'd had enough of trouble. Trouble seemed to come looking for him and he'd never been hard to find. His short-fused temper and confidence in his own ability to whip any man living were not designed to keep him out of trouble. If Luther Holcomb's trail led to trouble, he'd have a hard time remembering that he was a preacher now and not a roughneck brawler.

Dinner over, Trego tried to give his aunt some reassurance that he'd find Luther well and healthy. It twisted something inside him to see the hope spring into her eyes. It was like the hope of a drowning man grabbing at a straw. Trego's confidence in his own words was as hollow as the promise of safety offered by a straw drifting on a heavy sea. He had a gut feeling that Luther Holcomb was already dead or he'd have been home before this.

In the town of Sage Creek, Trego headed straight for the bank. He trusted his uncle; he'd give long odds that Luther had not taken Trego's money out of the bank before he left. But Trego had a long knife scar down his side as a reminder never to take anything or anybody for granted. He thought of his five thousand dollars, inherited from his preacher father and entrusted to his uncle. The possibility that it might be gone was ridiculous. Yet he had to know.

The shock of that inheritance still lingered with him. He'd grown up believing that preachers just didn't save any money. They didn't even make enough for any of the frills of living. Trego had accepted that. What he couldn't accept was the way his father had said nothing when people had cheated him, knowing he would not cause trouble, regardless of the pain it might bring to him and his destitute family.

Dan Trego had somehow scraped together enough money to send Sam to school so he could learn to be a preacher, too. But from the day he arrived at school, Sam had been determined that he would never be a preacher if that meant being shoved away from the good things of life.

His rebellion had grown as he went through school. After graduation, he had left school with the determination to prove that no one could run over him. He had proved it time and again until he was sick of proving it. He had found it wasn't something a man could prove once and the fact would stand without challenge. It had to be done each time a new challenge appeared.

Trego had never expected his father to own two dimes to rub together. Yet when he died a year ago, after being a widower for two years, his will showed that he still owned a piece of land he had bought when he preached in Omaha some years ago. Omaha had grown out to that land and when it was sold, it had brought five thousand dollars.

Trego had put that money in the care of his uncle because Luther had said he'd get together five thousand of his own money somehow and they'd buy a good ranch together. Of all the jobs Trego had held since leaving school, working on a ranch had appealed to him the most.

Now that he'd felt the urge to become the preacher his father had wanted him to be, Trego had hoped that he and his uncle could buy a ranch close to Sage Creek where Trego could preach in town on Sundays and work on the ranch through the week.

After Trego had identified himself to the teller in the bank, he asked for a statement of the balance in his uncle's account. While the teller looked up Luther's account, Trego turned and surveyed the lobby, leaning on the marble slab protruding from the sliding bars that separated the bank teller from the customers.

Two men had just come in, going directly to the back of the bank where the bank owner came out of his office to meet them.

"It's good to see you, Mr. Bridgewood," the banker said. "How are things up in Genesis?"

Trego's interest flared and he looked more closely at the visitors. The one called Mr. Bridgewood was rather short and carrying far too many pounds for his height. He wore a suit and a black hat that was dusty from travel. His stiff collar and black string tie made him look like a preacher dressed for church. His companion was a medium-sized man with a weathered, beaten-up hat and the flat-heeled work shoes of a farmer.

The teller returned to the window just then and Trego had to take his attention away from the two men from Genesis.

"Luther Holcomb has only sixty-two dollars and thirty cents in his account," the teller said.

Trego's brown eyes bored into the teller. "You've made a mistake," he said flatly. "He had a thousand or two of his own that I

15

know of. And he was keeping five thousand of my money."

"It's no mistake," the teller said defensively, scowling at Trego. "Luther Holcomb drew out seven thousand dollars two weeks ago. Took it all in twenty-dollar bills."

"What was he going to do with it?" Trego demanded.

"I don't know. It was his money and none of my business."

"It's some of mine!" Trego said, his eyes snapping. "Did he say where he was going?"

"Not a word. Men have taken their money and skipped out before."

Trego shot a hand under the bars of the window and caught the teller's shirt front in his fist like a mastiff grabbing a poodle. He jerked the man up against the window. "Not Uncle Luther!"

Gaining control of himself, he let go of the teller who fell back against a stool, gasping in amazement. Whirling on his heel, Trego started out of the bank. Was the teller right? Had Luther taken the money and skipped?

Suddenly Trego remembered the two men from Genesis. He turned that way, noting that they had stopped talking to stare at him. He had made a spectacle of himself. It hadn't been the teller's fault if he was tell-

16

ing the truth and Trego had no real reason to doubt him.

The three men jerked their eyes away from Trego when he turned their way and the Sage Creek banker asked the short heavy man what he was doing down here.

"Tom and I are looking for a minister for our church. Our preacher was killed in a tragic accident when his buggy ran off the road and into a canyon."

Trego barely heard what the man said. He touched the heavy man's sleeve. "Did you say you are from Genesis?"

The man turned, his piercing blue eyes probing into Trego. "That's right. I don't believe we've met before."

"We haven't," Trego said. "I'm looking for my uncle, Luther Holcomb. I think he may have gone to your town."

Bridgewood shook his head. "We have a young couple, Pace and Katie Holcomb, living there. But no Luther Holcomb."

"Pace is my cousin," Trego said. "Luther is his father. He's been gone from here for two weeks. His wife is mighty worried."

Bridgewood nodded. "I can understand." He turned to the man with him. "Have you heard of Luther Holcomb, Tom?"

The other man shook his head and turned soft blue eyes on Trego. "Pace Holcomb

17

lives right next to me. If his father had come to visit, I'm sure he would have told me."

Trego sized up the two men. Both had open faces that he could trust.

The heavy man stuck out a hand. "I'm Ivan Bridgewood. I have a bank in Genesis. This is Tom Ekhart, a homesteader on the other side of Ash Creek Canyon from town."

Trego shook hands with the men. "My name is Sam Trego." He started to say he'd been working on the railroad then his memory recalled hearing Bridgewood say that they were looking for a minister. He had barely paid any attention to that when he'd heard it. "I'm a preacher," he said, finding the words strange to his tongue.

"Well now," Bridgewood said with a smile. "We're looking for a preacher. We have a little community church in our town." His eyes ran up and down Trego and his smile spread across his face. "You're the biggest preacher I ever saw. Maybe you can scare the devil out of some of those hellions if you can't talk it out of them."

Trego shrugged and grinned. "I've scared the devil out of a lot of people, but it wasn't with preaching."

"Would you be interested in preaching for a while at our church?" Bridgewood asked. "The pay isn't much but we have a good parsonage right beside the church. Come for a month's trial. If you like the job and we like you, we'll make it a permanent arrangement."

Trego hadn't expected to get a job almost before he'd fully made up his mind to preach. But he'd already decided to go to Genesis. It was the logical place to begin looking for Luther. He'd find him and that money if he had to turn the world upside down.

"I'll take you up on that," Trego said.

Tom Ekhart was studying Trego with squinting eyes. "Are you coming to preach or to look for your uncle?" he demanded.

Trego met his stare. "Both. I won't fool you. My first concern is to find my uncle. My aunt thinks he went to Genesis and that seems logical since his son lives there. I'll preach at your church but I'm also going to find out if my uncle went there and what happened to him if he did."

"Fair enough," Bridgewood said amiably.

Ekhart rubbed his chin thoughtfully. "Just a word of caution," he said. "Strangers are rare in Genesis."

Trego couldn't mistake the warning in Ekhart's words.

# 2

"Just what do you mean by that?" Trego asked.

"I don't know what's going on," Ekhart said slowly. "But when Mr. Bridgewood and I were in Primrose yesterday looking for a preacher, I talked to a man named Wilson. He has a cousin living near Genesis. He started over to visit him not long ago and was turned back just before he got to Genesis."

"Why would anyone turn back a visitor to Genesis?" Trego asked, his interest kindling and his determination to get to Genesis growing.

"I have no idea. Neither does Wilson. He was just going for a visit. Let me suggest that if anybody stops you, tell them you're a preacher, not someone going to visit friends or relatives."

"You're blowing things out of all proportion, Tom," Bridgewood chided softly.

"Maybe," Ekhart said. "But there's something strange going on. I don't want our new preacher to be taken by surprise."

"I don't intend to be," Trego said.

Trego considered going back to the farm and telling his aunt what he had learned and where he was going but decided against it. He didn't want to have to tell her that Luther had taken almost all their money out of the bank. What little was left wouldn't last Ruth very long.

Bridgewood invited Trego to ride back to Genesis with Ekhart and him in their spring wagon but Trego refused. He wanted to go alone. He had some thinking to do and he wasn't sure just what he was riding into. It might be well to remain totally neutral until he saw how things stacked up. He carried a painful memory of the time he had taken sides before he had learned about both outfits and he'd found himself on the wrong side.

Before setting out, Trego went to the store and bought enough food to last him several days. He debated about strapping on his gun before starting for Genesis, but decided against that. He wouldn't be able to convince many people he was a preacher if he was wearing a gun.

At sundown, he made camp near the stage

road. The last time he'd been at Sage Creek there hadn't been anything between there and Hawk's Nest except a few stage stations. Genesis was apparently an outgrowth of one of those stations. It was a lonely uninhabited land between Sage Creek and Hawk's Nest, a huge dry land so slashed up by canyons that it discouraged settlement. The branch stage line across this canyon country was the only connection between the valley where Sage Creek lay and the railroad to the north.

Trego was up at dawn and fed his horse some oats to go with the grass he had found during the night. Saddling up, he moved out on the road. He had never been up this road and he was amazed at the depth of the canyons that cut this rolling plain into narrow strips. The flat land could probably be farmed if there was enough rain.

The stage road threaded its way between the canyons, crossing one only when absolutely necessary. In only a few places was that even possible. It was the canyons that intrigued Trego. Wonderful pasture was down there for cattle with enough trees for shade. And if there was any water anywhere in this semi-arid country, it would be in the bottoms of those canyons. Buffalo and grama grass covered the flat plains, but there was bunch grass on the slopes of the canyons. He passed one stage station early in the morning and another one about the middle of the forenoon.

It wasn't quite noon when Trego found the road dipping across a swale that ran into a canyon to his right. He was at the bottom of the swale when two men nudged horses out from behind a bank to his right. Each had a gun in his hand.

"Where are you going, mister?" one demanded.

Trego halted, glaring at the two men. If ever there was a contrast between men, it was here. One was as big as a skinned cow with dark brown, almost black hair and eyes to match. The other was little bigger than a large boy with sandy hair and slate-colored eyes. Trego immediately tagged the little one as more dangerous with a gun. A small man did his fighting with a gun; a big man was more apt to use his fists and strength.

"I'm heading for Genesis," Trego said. "Something you want?"

"Maybe," the little man said. "Who are you going to see there?"

"I'm the new preacher," Trego said, recalling what Ekhart had told him.

The two men exchanged glances. "We ain't needing no preachers, either," the bigger one said. "Let's send him back."

"He don't look to me like the kind you send anywhere," the little man said. "Shall we hang him or shoot him?"

The big man seemed to consider that question carefully. "Hang him," he said finally.

The little man grinned. "By the thumbs. So his toes can barely touch the ground."

Trego began to realize the seriousness of his situation. He didn't doubt that the little man would do exactly what he was suggesting. His faded eyes were as evil as any Trego had ever seen, and he had seen his share in the last few years. This man would thoroughly enjoy torturing him.

Trego mentally lashed himself for putting his gun in his saddle bags. Once these two had him strung up under the limb of some tree, he'd stand there until he died. There wasn't much traffic on this road and nobody would look into the canyons as they passed. These two men would have to take him down into a canyon to find a tree where they could hang him.

Probably they intended to rob him, too. Maybe this was the fate that Luther Holcomb had met. Trego had always been able to get out of any tight spot, mainly because of his size and strength. But with a gun prodding his belly, he wouldn't have much chance of getting out of this one.

"Get down," the little man with the slate eyes said, motioning with the gun muzzle.

Rebellion surged through Trego, but he realized that could be fatal. Glaring at the little man, he swung down. Trego towered over him when he was on the ground but the gun the slate-eyed man held made him the bigger.

"What now?" the other gunman asked.

"Ground hitch his horse," his partner said. "Then we'll take him down to the trees."

Trego saw the big man flip the reins from around the horse's neck and drop a good-sized rock on the ends. Then he turned to Trego, prodding him in the back with his gun muzzle. Trego started down the ravine reluctantly, watching for a chance to make a break. But the little man stayed a dozen steps behind his partner, his gun ready to cut short any attempt at escape. If it had been the little man directly behind him, Trego might have tried to make a move on him, hoping to conquer him before his big partner could get into the action. But Trego knew he could never move fast enough to escape the little outlaw's reaction.

They found a good-sized ash tree less than sixty yards down the ravine around a slight bend, out of sight of the road. The little man called a halt there.

"This is good enough. Nobody will see him here."

"How are you going to make a rope stay on his thumbs?" the big man asked, fingering the rope in his hand.

"Can't," the little man said. "Just tie the rope around his wrists. His hands won't slip through the noose."

The big man slipped a noose over Trego's hands while the little man held a cocked revolver on him. Throwing the rope over a fairly high limb, the big man pulled it over to another big limb, tightening it till Trego's toes barely touched the ground. The little man moved over to make sure the rope was securely tied. Stepping back, he surveyed their work.

"We ain't really leaving you to die," he said. "Maybe you can slide that rope along the limb until you get enough slack to slip your hands out of that noose." He grinned like a well-fed cat. "By that time, you should have enough sense to get out of the country."

The two turned and hurried up the ravine, disappearing from Trego's view. Trego stared up at the limb above his head. It ran almost parallel to the ground and Trego was already standing on tiptoes. There was no way he could get enough slack to slide the rope along the limb toward the tree trunk. The little man had known that. Trego heard horses moving up on the road. The two must have had their horses hidden close to the road and they were probably taking Trego's horse, too. Everything he had was in that bedroll. Not that it really made any difference now.

Trego tried to move the rope along the limb by jumping up and lunging forward. All he accomplished was to jerk his arms almost out of their sockets and nearly tear his hands off at the wrists. He couldn't see that the rope had moved a bit. His fingers and arms were growing numb from lack of circulation. He tried to ease his frustration by picturing the two men who had done this. If he ever saw them again, together or separately, he'd know them. He tried not to think of the odds against his living to see them again, and revelled in the satisfaction he'd get out of breaking every bone in their bodies. He ached all over from standing on tiptoe to ease the strain of stretched muscles, but most of the agony centered in his arms and shoulders.

Time seemed to stand still as the hot afternoon wore on. Vaguely he thought that

27

he was lucky to be in the shade of a tree. He wanted to laugh or cry, he wasn't sure which, just thinking that anything about his present situation could be lucky. Was he losing his mind? It was possible, he supposed, under these circumstances.

When he first heard the clump of hoofbeats on the road above him, he thought it was an illusion. But the sounds persisted and he forced his wandering mind to concentrate on them. Someone was actually going along the road. But what good was that going to do him? They couldn't see him down here. He tried to yell but only made a hoarse croak. He summoned all his strength and forced it into a yell. This time the sound resembled a yell. It was his fourth shout that brought a halt to the sound of moving horses. Into that silence, he screamed his loudest. Then he waited.

He thought that if the horses went on, he'd just give up and die. It would be easier that way. But when the sound above him resumed, it wasn't horses moving but the swish of someone walking through grass.

A man and a woman came in sight of the tree and stopped to stare at him. He wanted to shout again but his throat felt too dry to make another sound. The man finally came on.

"Who did that?" he demanded, making no move to get Trego down. "Who are you?"

"An idiot," Trego whispered, "to let anyone do this. I never saw the men before. Get me down."

The man nodded as though debating his next move. Then he went to the limb where the rope was tied and fumbled with the knot.

"It's too tight," he said. "I need some slack."

The woman came forward. In spite of his misery, Trego was aware that she was very young, probably half the age of the man. She was dressed well with a wide-brimmed hat pinned to her head by long hatpins through her hair and wearing a flowered blouse and divided skirt.

"Let me do it, Horace," she said. She pulled a knife from a sheath at the top of her boot and began sawing on the rope.

The man, barely as tall as the girl but a little heavier, tipped his head back to watch her work. His hat fell off, revealing a bald head.

The girl sawed vigorously for what seemed like an eternity to Trego before the rope gave way. His arms dropped. He found that his legs wouldn't hold him and he crumpled in a heap. The girl was at his side in an instant.

"Are you shot?" she asked, loosening the noose and sliding the rope off his hands.

He shook his head, disgusted at his weakness. "Been standing on my toes too long, I guess. I'll be all right as soon as I get the quiver out of my legs."

The little man had recovered his hat and planted it firmly back on his head. "Now, we'd like to know who we rescued," he said.

"Sam Trego. I was on my way to Genesis." Trego looked at his saviors. "I sure want to thank you for taking a load off my arms."

"I'm Horace Dibble, the druggist in Genesis," the man said, holding out his hand. "This is Alvena Oyler, daughter of the storekeeper in town."

Trego tried to lift his hand to grasp Dibble's, but couldn't do it. The druggist reached down and gripped his hand.

"Do you know who did this?" Dibble asked.

"A big slob of a man and a little man with colorless eyes. I'll know them if I ever see them again."

"I can't think of anybody fitting that description," Dibble said. "I've heard of a gang of outlaws called the Winchester Gang that is supposed to be in this area. Perhaps you had the bad luck to bump into them."

"It was bad luck, all right," Trego said. He got up carefully and tried to stand, but his legs wobbled until he staggered to the tree trunk and leaned against it. "I've got a horse up on the road."

The druggist shook his head. "Maybe you did have. There's none there now."

"I suppose they stole that, too," Trego said.

"Why were you going to Genesis?" Alvena asked. "Do you know somebody there?"

Trego frowned. That was the second time today he'd been asked that question. The first time he'd been hanged by the hands for his answer. How could he be sure these two hadn't been sent back by those men to try to get answers they had failed to get? This girl and the little bald-headed man didn't look vicious. But they didn't need to be. Right now he couldn't whip a ten-year-old boy.

# 3

"I'm a preacher," Trego said finally, watching the two closely. "I heard there was a church without a preacher in Genesis."

"There is," Alvena said eagerly. "We'll take you on to Genesis. You can ride my horse."

Trego shot a look at Dibble, the druggist. He seemed about to object, then changed his mind. "He'll ride my horse," he said. "Walking won't hurt me."

"It won't hurt me, either, if I can do it," Trego said.

With Dibble holding one arm and Alvena the other, Trego staggered up the ravine to the road. Dibble helped Trego onto the saddle of one of the two horses, then took the reins and led it up the road. Alvena rode directly behind him. Trego barely had strength enough to hold himself in the saddle.

"There are people in and around Genesis who don't seem to want a preacher here,"

Dibble said after they had gone some distance.

"Meaning that I'd be a fool to stay here and preach?" Trego asked.

"I don't think so," Alvena said quickly. "Most of us want a preacher. There may be outlaws around but that was just a freak accident that killed Mr. Knowles."

Trego said nothing. Knowles was the preacher who had died in the accident that Bridgewood had told him about, his rig going off into a canyon. Obviously Horace Dibble didn't think it was an accident. Maybe Alvena didn't, either. Trego couldn't imagine why anyone would have a grudge against preachers. There was something out of whack here.

It was late afternoon when they reached the town. For the last mile, the road had followed the rim of a canyon running from northwest to the southeast. Then a bend in the canyon straightened its direction to due north and the town sat on the east rim. It wasn't much of a town. To Trego, it looked much like he'd expect a stage station to look after it had exploded into a town. There were businesses and homes intermingled up and down the one street. Only on the east side were there houses back of the main street. The canyon was too close on the west for additional buildings.

They turned in at the livery barn, the first place of business on the south end of town. The corral behind the barn ran right out to the lip of the canyon. Across the street from the barn was a blacksmith shop and a little house to the north of that. That would be the parsonage that Bridgewood had told him about.

"That's my drugstore up the street north of the church," Dibble said. "And that's Cal Oyler's general store to the north of my store."

Trego saw a fairly large house between the parsonage and Dibble's store, and he noticed a couple of houses back of the business places. On the canyon side of the street were several buidings with a bank at the far end across from Oyler's store. Just north of the livery barn, was a big building that Trego guessed was a hotel or boardinghouse.

"Feel like walking?" Dibble asked, as he helped Trego down.

The numbness that had rendered him almost helpless had worn off as he rode into town and Trego was determined that he wouldn't ask for any more help. "I can manage all right," he said.

"I want you to meet some of the people in

town," Dibble said. "Roger Sorenson runs this livery barn. He's not far from your age. He doesn't seem to be here right now. Come on over and meet the blacksmith."

"Jumbo isn't interested in church," Alvena said.

"With the church right next to him, he should be," Dibble said.

The blacksmith, Jumbo Furtak, stepped to the door when Dibble called. Trego was shocked at his size and looks. He wasn't quite as tall as Trego, but he was heavier and every ounce looked to be solid muscle. A man that size ought to have the dark hair of a buffalo, but Furtak's hair was almost white and his eyes a faded gray. He wasn't much older than Trego. Furtak wiped his grimy hands on his pants before shaking hands. Trego squeezed hard to match the huge man's grip.

Dibble led the way back across the street toward the boardinghouse. Trego looked over the two-story building. He'd be seeing a lot of that because it was directly across the main street from the church and parsonage. It was almost square with four identical sections of roof sloping down from a three-foot square at the center that had an iron railing around it. That square made Trego think of a lookout station built to hold a guard watching for enemies.

Just to the north of the boardinghouse was a small building that had a little sign above the door that said "Office of the Deputy Sheriff." Apparently Dibble wanted him to meet the law in Genesis, too.

Fred Petrauk was a short man, far too heavy for his height, with hair like faded straw and eyes the color of a clear sky. His handshake was as limp as Furtak's had been powerful. Petrauk didn't strike Trego as looking much like a law officer. Trego was still thinking of him as they stepped back out into the street. There they met a man hurrying down the street from the north. He was a small, dark-haired man who appeared to be a bundle of nerves.

"Cal!" Dibble exclaimed. "I was just bringing a man up to see you who wants the job of preacher. Alvena has practically hired him without giving anybody else a chance to say a word."

"We need a preacher, Pa," Alvena said. "Mr. Trego will make a good one."

Cal Oyler looked sharply from Trego to his daughter, his eyes nervously probing like an inquisitive boy examining a snake with a stick. "How do you know?"

"I just do," Alvena said. "A growing town needs a preacher."

"That's right," Oyler agreed, still sizing up Trego.

Trego thought of telling them he had already been hired, but he was still reluctant to give out any information that he didn't have to. Something was definitely wrong here at Genesis, and the less he said about himself until he found out what it was, the safer he'd be.

"I'm going over and look at the parsonage," he said, turning toward the little house next to the white church.

The church was not big but it would hold all that he could get to come to services from this small community. It had a tall belfry, but he saw no bell in the top. The paint was bright as befitted a building that was fairly new. In fact, he didn't see any building in town that looked old unless it was Oyler's store. That had probably been the stage station before the town blossomed here. He was almost across the street before he realized that Alvena was coming with him. He shot a questioning look at her.

"You'll need someone to help you clean up the place," she said defensively. "Our former preacher, Oliver Knowles, was a bachelor and he didn't keep house too well."

"I hope you don't expect me to do any better," Trego said.

Alvena giggled and ran ahead of him to push open the unlocked door. The interior wasn't as littered as he had expected it to be. It looked as if someone had simply walked out and not returned, which was probably exactly what had happened.

"There must be some settlers around here I can depend on to come to church," Trego said.

"There are several homesteaders," Alvena replied. "Most of them are to the southwest across Ash Creek Canyon. It's flat land over there, good farmland."

"Who lives there?"

"Pace Holcomb has the first place. Then there's Tom Ekhart and Web Myrick. Beyond them, on the other side of Spring Canyon, is Quint Guzek's ZK ranch. There are three homesteads on that ranch. Makes Guzek furious when he talks about it. Our deputy, Fred Petrauk, used to work for Guzek. He took one homestead and the two men he has working for him, Dett Skeen and Grumpy Rush, have also taken homesteads there. They used to work for Guzek, too."

Trego realized he had tapped a fountain of information. He hoped he could store it all in his mind and sort it out as he got acquainted with the people here. Somewhere there might be a clue to Luther Holcomb's whereabouts. His first job tomorrow would be to go see his cousin, Pace. Pace would surely know something about Luther. Tonight, he'd just get to bed as soon as he had it ready. He was sure that by tomorrow, he'd feel like starting his real work here.

He thanked Alvena for her help then started making the bed with clean sheets he found on a shelf. Before he had finished, Alvena was back with some groceries from her father's store. Trego had been so tired he hadn't even thought of food. What he had brought had disappeared along with his gun and his horse.

An idea struck him and he asked Alvena if she recognized the men who had jumped him from the description he had given.

"Maybe," she said. "I'm not sure. If they are the ones I'm guessing, they usually loaf around in the back room of Mr. Dibble's drugstore when they're in town. That's most of the time."

"I'll check tomorrow," he said. "I want to get my horse back."

He slept the sleep of the weary. He didn't even bother to notice whether the bed was comfortable or not. He found himself slightly stiff the next morning, but little the worse otherwise for his experience of the day before. After eating a good breakfast, he tried lifting and reaching, finding that his arms and legs were in reasonably good shape. He intended to visit Dibble's back room and if he found the two men who had robbed and hanged him yesterday, he wanted to be in shape to enforce his demand that he get his horse and equipment back. He thought of riding out to Pace Holcomb's before noon, but decided that his first job was to get his own horse back. He didn't want to have to rent a horse every time he left town.

He waited impatiently, his determination growing, until after dinner. Then he decided that the two men would be in Dibble's back room now if they were going to be there today. As he walked up the street, he wondered what was in Dibble's back room that made it so attractive to people.

Just to the north of the parsonage was a huge house, surely the fanciest home in Genesis. As he passed, he saw Ivan Bridgewood in the yard behind the house, probably doing some noon chores before going back to the bank. Trego hadn't shown himself all morning so Bridgewood probably didn't know that he was here yet. It was nice to have the banker for a close neighbor.

At Dibble's drugstore, he turned into the false-fronted building. Dibble was close to his shelf of medicine and he came over, a big smile on his face. A heavy-chested, pure white bulldog stood in front of the counter, glaring malevolently at Trego.

"Glad to see you this morning, Reverend," Dibble said, holding out his hand.

Trego gripped it, but shook his head. "Better save that 'reverend' till I have a look at your back room."

Dibble's smile faded a little. "I have a party room back there. I sell a few spirits and there are tables for card games. I doubt if there is anything in there that would interest you."

"I want to see for myself," Trego said, and pushed past the druggist to the partition door. He opened it quietly.

His eyes fell on the back of the huge man who had helped hang him from the tree limb yesterday. Right beside him, also with his back to Trego, was his little partner.

"This is no place for a preacher," Dibble said gently at Trego's elbow.

"Right now I don't feel much like a preacher," Trego said softly. "Those two are the ones who robbed me yesterday and hung me from that tree."

"Don't push them," Dibble whispered.

41

"They're bad medicine."

"I'm not so good myself," Trego said.

Trego stepped inside. With the swiftness of a striking snake, he grabbed the gun out of the little man's holster. The man wheeled, knocking the gun into the corner. That was all right with Trego. The little man was unarmed now.

The big man whirled at the disturbance, his eyes popping when he saw Trego. His partner dodged away from Trego and stopped half behind the big man.

"Get him, Grumpy," he commanded.

Suddenly it struck Trego who these men were. Alvena had said that the two men who worked for the deputy were Grumpy Rush and Dett Skeen. These must be the two. Right now he didn't care if they were deputy sheriffs themselves.

"I want my horse back with everything that was on him," Trego said.

"And what if you don't get him?" Skeen sneered, moving a little farther behind Grumpy's bulk.

White hot rage swept through Trego. He'd felt it many times before and he knew what the results would be. At this moment, he didn't care. "Either I get my horse and my things or there'll be two new graves in town. Your choice."

42

Skeen recoiled, glancing around for his gun. Grumpy simply stood there, apparently not believing what he was seeing and hearing. Trego glanced at the bar along one wall. Two men stood there, watching expectantly, showing no inclination to join the argument.

"Where's my horse?" Trego demanded, stepping closer to the big man.

"Get him, Grumpy!" Skeen squeaked. "He'll kill you if you don't."

Grumpy lashed out with a big fist. Trego had expected it. In the minute he'd been here, he saw that Skeen was not only the more dangerous of the two, but he was the brains as well. Trego was going to have his hands full now.

Grumpy Rush was just as strong as Trego had suspected. But he was an alley fighter, confident he could crush an opponent by sheer weight and force. Trego was equally confident he could handle a man like Grumpy. But he had the added worry of Dett Skeen. Although Skeen was not a physical fighter, he was treacherous. Skeen had been disarmed but he might get his gun again while Trego was battling Grumpy.

Trego stepped out of the way of Grumpy's charge and slammed a fist into his face as he went past. Even as he landed that blow, he saw Skeen begin inching toward the wall where his gun had skittered. Trego couldn't afford the luxury of whittling Grumpy down with the tactical moves of boxing. He'd have to get Grumpy out of the fight as quickly as possible.

When Grumpy charged again, Trego held his ground and exchanged blows with him. That was what Grumpy had wanted but now he discovered that here was a man he couldn't run over. Grumpy was almost as heavy as Trego; at six foot two, he was three inches shorter and his arms were not quite as long.

A table stood behind Grumpy where a card game had been forming when Trego came in. Trego caught Grumpy in the midsection and drove him backward into the table. The table skidded for a foot then collapsed under Grumpy. Before the big man could get back to his feet, Trego wheeled to locate Skeen. Skeen was over by the wall now, just stooping to pick up the gun. When he got it in his hand, Trego would be as good as dead.

# 4

Trego leaped toward Skeen, knocking two chairs out of his way. He reached the wall just as Skeen was rising, gripping the gun. Trego's fist caught the little man on the side of the head and he flew backward like a batted ball, hitting the wall with a thud, his elbow jamming through the one window in the room. He slid down the wall in a heap, his head sagging to one side, looking like a discarded rag doll. Trego didn't expect him to get back into this fight.

But Grumpy was back in it. He had regained his feet and was charging toward Trego with all the fury of a mad bull. He wasn't accustomed to being manhandled and he hadn't lost his confidence that he could whip any man. With Skeen momentarily out of the way, Trego turned to meet Grumpy with an eagerness he thought he had put behind him. He had his chance now to avenge those hours he had stood on tiptoe to keep his arms from being pulled out of their sockets.

They met like a couple of mountain rams, each bent on the complete destruction of his opponent. Then Trego stepped aside suddenly and smashed a fist against the side of Grumpy's head. Grumpy was whirled around and caught himself by grabbing the back of a chair. The chair withstood the strain for a moment, then crumpled under Grumpy's weight. Again he went down.

Trego waited for him to get up, having blotted out all memory of his resolution not to get into any more fights. He was thoroughly enjoying his moment of revenge.

Grumpy got up again, his eyes slightly glazed as he stared at Trego. Once more he charged and Trego stepped aside, chopping a fist against the man's head. Grumpy turned and Trego caught him full in the face with a powerful blow. Grumpy went down and this time he didn't try to get up. Trego backed to the wall and leaned against it. Skeen appeared to be out cold against the adjoining wall. Trego's eyes turned toward the partition doorway.

Dibble was staring at the two men on the floor and at the broken table, chair, and window. His face had lost its color. Cal

Oyler was beside him, apparently having heard the noise from his store just to the north.

"I thought you were a holy man," Oyler said softly, staring at Trego.

"He's a holy terror!" Dibble breathed. "Look at what he did!"

"They started it yesterday when they hung me by my hands," Trego said. He reached down and caught Grumpy by the shirt front. "Where's my horse?"

Grumpy only groaned. Trego shook him and repeated the question. Grumpy scowled, making no effort to get up. "You ain't got no horse."

Trego jerked him to his knees. "I want that horse!"

Grumpy squirmed. "Let go. You're hurting me."

"Tell me where my horse is or you'll find out what hurting really means."

Grumpy writhed in Trego's grasp then muttered, "He's in Dett's barn."

Trego dropped Grumpy like a sack of wheat. He didn't doubt that Grumpy had told the truth. According to what Alvena had said, Dett Skeen's homestead was on Guzek's ZK ranch out beyond Spring Canyon.

Dibble suddenly broke away from the

47

doorway and Trego wheeled to see where he was going. Dibble reached Skeen's gun just before the revived gunman could get to it.

"There's been enough damage here without you shooting somebody," Dibble snapped.

Trego realized he owed Dibble for that. He had almost forgotten Skeen. He turned toward the door. "Thanks, Mr. Dibble," he said.

"What about the damage here?" Dibble asked.

"Take it out of their hides if they've got it," Trego said. "If they haven't, I'll see you later and make a settlement."

He went on through the drugstore and out into the street. Going down the sidewalk, he turned in at the parsonage. He had more bruises than he cared to admit. Grumpy Rush was no slouch of a fighter even if he had no finesse. But it was Dett Skeen he'd have to watch. If it hadn't been for Horace Dibble, he might be dead right now.

He washed his face, holding the soothing water· on the bruises, then dried off and went outside again. He crossed the street and had turned toward the livery barn when the overweight deputy sheriff came from his office just to the north of the boarding-house.

"Heard you smashed up Dibble's place," he said.

"You heard wrong," Trego said. "I smashed up a couple of thieves who stole my horse and goods yesterday. They smashed the furniture when they fell."

Petrauk rubbed his chin. "Nobody ever pushes Grumpy around."

"I don't recall pushing him. But I sure knocked him around."

Trego spun away. He didn't feel like another fight now, especially against a man wearing a star. As he turned away, Trego saw Dett Skeen's face in the window of the deputy's office. He knew then how Petrauk had found out so quickly about the fight at Dibble's. He half expected Petrauk to push the issue, but he didn't.

At the barn, Trego found Roger Sorenson. Sorenson was of average size and average appearance, the kind of man who could lose himself in a crowd of half a dozen people.

"I want to rent a horse for the afternoon," Trego said.

"Got a good one here, Preacher," Sorenson said. "I was told you were here last night. I was out seeing my girl, Amy Green. We're going to be married soon. We'll want you to tie the knot."

Trego nodded. "I'll look forward to it. How far is it out to Dett Skeen's place?"

"About three miles. But he's in town. At least, he came in this morning."

"It's his place, not him, that I want to see," Trego said. "He's got my horse out there. Do I take this road to the southwest?"

Sorenson nodded. "You'll come to Holcomb's first. Then Ekhart's and Myrick's. Then you cross Spring Canyon. Petrauk's place is right on the road. Skeen has a place off to the right about a quarter of a mile."

Trego took the horse and headed out of town. He hoped his possessionns were still with his horse. He had the uneasy feeling he was going to need that gun, even if he was a preacher now.

The road turned southwest just south of Sorenson's barn and followed a ravine that dropped down to the bottom of Ash Creek Canyon, which hemmed in the town on the west. The road was steep, but it was the only place near town where a wagon could get down into the bottom of the canyon. The floor of the canyon was a quarter of a mile wide, lush with good grass. Ash and cottonwood trees lined the little stream cutting down the center of the canyon. This would make a wonderful winter pasture for cattle,

Trego thought, or even a good farm, providing floods didn't sweep down the canyon too often.

The road up the other side was a longer, more gentle slope. He broke out on a fairly flat plain that stretched ahead for nearly two miles. On the left side he saw a house. According to what he'd been told, that would be Pace Holcomb's homestead. He needed to see Pace and find out what he knew about Luther. Getting his horse would have to wait. He reined down the lane leading from the road. Both the house and the barn were of sod. The barn had a pole roof while the house had a board, tarpaper, and sod roof. He swung down in front of the house.

Pace Holcomb came from the barn at the same time that Katie appeared at the door. Pace recognized him immediately and came on the run.

"Sam!" he exclaimed. "It's sure good to see you. Haven't seen anyone from home for ages."

He gripped Trego's hand while the big man looked from Pace to Katie. "Haven't you seen your father?"

"No," Pace said. "Why would he come here?"

"I don't know," Trego admitted. "But your mother thought he did. He's been gone from home for two weeks."

Pace frowned, his brown eyes clouded with worry. "We sure haven't seen him. What are you doing here?"

"Looking for Luther, for one thing. I'm also the preacher in town."

"A preacher?" Pace exclaimed. "I thought you said you weren't going to be a preacher."

"I changed my mind. I was told they needed a preacher here. Besides, I hear that strangers with no business in Genesis aren't made very welcome."

Katie had come out to greet Trego. "I've heard that, too," she said. "Something is wrong around here."

"I was held up and robbed of my horse and possessions as I came in," Trego said. "I just found out where my horse is and I'm going after him now. Don't let anybody know that we're related. If something has happened to Uncle Luther, they'd figure out in a hurry that I am here to look for him."

"We won't breathe a word," Katie promised. "But we will be at church tomorrow to hear you preach."

Trego mounted his rented horse again. "When was the last time you heard from your folks?"

"A long time ago," Pace said. "We've been thinking we'd ought to go over to Sage Creek and see why they haven't written."

Trego nodded. "Aunt Ruth says she has written. Why didn't you write her?"

"We have," Katie said. "But we don't get any answer."

"Something odd really is going on," Trego said. "I'll see you at church tomorrow."

He headed on west, passing two more homesteads, one on either side of the road, before coming to another canyon. This canyon wasn't as deep as the one near town but it was narrower and the road down into it and up the other side was steeper.

Again he came out on fairly level land. Not far ahead was a small sod house on the right side of the road. That would be Petrauk's place. He rode past it and turned his horse off to the right toward a low sod house some distance back from the road. There was another low sod building behind the house. Trego went directly to it and found his horse inside. It took a couple of minutes to find his saddle, which was under some sacks in the corner. His bedroll was still tied behind the cantle. A quick examination satisfied him that nothing had been taken from it.

Saddling his horse, he led him out of the

barn, mounted and, leading the livery horse, headed back toward town. Crossing Spring Canyon, he stopped at the middle of the three places between there and town. According to what he'd been told, this would be Tom Ekhart's place.

Tom Ekhart had a frame house instead of sod as the others had but his barn and shed were sod. A wagon and team stood in the yard when Trego reined up. Ekhart himself came out of the house. A rather tall man followed him.

"Glad to see you, Preacher," Ekhart said. "I want you to meet one of your flock, Web Myrick. Lives a piece up the road toward Spring Canyon."

Trego dismounted and shook Myrick's hand. He liked the appearance of Web Myrick.

"Taking to traveling with two horses, Preacher?" Ekhart asked.

"My horse was stolen yesterday as I was coming to Genesis," Trego explained. "I just found out where he was so I went after him."

Ekhart grinned. "I heard how you learned where he was. That was the first I knew you were even in the country."

"How did you hear?" Trego asked.

"Quint and Yonnie Guzek just came by.

They'd been in town. If anything happens within two miles of Yonnie, she hears about it. And then she tells everybody she sees. Sometimes she doctors the story up a bit, too."

Trego recognized the name. The Guzeks owned the ZK ranch where Petrauk and his two hired hands had homesteaded. "Is she a gossip?" he asked.

"They don't call her Yawn-ie for nothing," Ekhart said, grinning. "She's always got her mouth open talking."

"She was mighty pleased with the way you took care of Rush and Skeen," Myrick said. "She'd love a rabid coyote more than she does those two."

"I heard that they took homesteads on Guzek's land," Trego said.

"Old Quint also thinks they're stocking their land with ZK cattle," Ekhart added. "I wouldn't be surprised if he's right. Yonnie heard how you'd been robbed and tied up on your way here. I hope you won't let this introduction to our country scare you out."

"I don't scare easy," Trego said. He almost added that he'd not be run out until he found out whether his uncle had come here, but then he looked at Web Myrick and decided against it. He didn't know Myrick, and the fewer people who knew what he was really here for, the safer he'd be.

A girl in a checkered gingham dress with a white apron appeared in the doorway behind Tom Ekhart, but she darted back inside like a frightened prairie dog only to appear a moment later without the apron. Trego watched her in fascination. He had seen a lot of pretty girls in the last few years. Alvena Oyler was one of them. But this girl overshadowed them all. Her auburn hair caught the afternoon sun, reflecting a copper glint. Her deep blue eyes were framed in a heart shaped face, accented by her rather high cheek bones. She was a small girl by any standards, but she looked exceptionally tiny from Trego's commanding height.

Ekhart noticed Trego's stare and turned. "This is my daughter, Vona. Our new preacher, Sam Trego."

Trego acknowledged the introduction and the girl came forward, the rosy blush in her cheeks heightened by more than just the sun's glow. "Mama wants to know if you will stay for supper," she said.

"Thanks for the invitation," Trego said. "But I'd better get this horse back to the livery stable. I've got to get a sermon ready for tomorrow, too. Haven't had much time to think about that."

Her eyes dropped. "We'll be at church tomorrow," she said, and scurried back into the house.

Trego took his leave and headed on toward town. He did have things to do, but now his mind was distracted by the picture of a soft heart-shaped face with deep blue eyes, tiny nose, and ripe lips. How was he going to concentrate on a sermon with that picture in his mind?

After returning the rented horse and making arrangements to keep his own horse in the livery barn, Trego went to the parsonage. There was a paper tied to the knob of his door. The picture of Vona Ekhart was wiped out of his mind when he read what was printed on the paper.

"Try to preach tomorrow and somebody will be preaching your funeral."

Trego was sure he knew who had put that note there. But what could he do about it? Standing in a pulpit preaching, he'd be a perfect target for anybody mad enough to kill him. Trego didn't doubt that Dett Skeen was.

Horace Dibble came down the street just before dark with his bulldog on a leash. He stopped in front of the parsonage. Trego stepped outside.

"How do you feel after the fight?" the

druggist asked.

"I've got a few bruises, but I'll survive. Did you get paid for the damage to your place?"

"I made arrangements with Dett and Grumpy." Dibble grinned. "It was worth something to me to see somebody handle that big bear. Grumpy thought he could whip anything on two feet." The dog tried to go out into the street and Dibble braced himself to pull him back.

"That's quite a dog you have," Trego said.

"I'm a bachelor, you know," Dibble said. "King keeps me company and he's a good watchdog. Nobody will bother my store while he is on guard."

Trego nodded. "I can believe that. See you in church tomorrow?"

"You can count on me," Dibble said, and let the bulldog lead him on down the street.

Trego went back inside and tried to settle down to getting his sermon ready. He had preached a sermon while in school on brotherly love. That ought to be a good one here where there seemed to be a need for that commodity among some people.

Apprehension gripped Trego as he prepared to go over to the church the next morning. He strapped on his gun belt before he left. He had never worn a gun to

58

church before, but church here in Genesis was going to be different from any he'd ever attended.

The church was small with rows of benches for seats. The pulpit was a crudely built affair, but it was big and Trego appreciated that. There was a chair behind the pulpit and he seated himself in that and went over the few notes for his sermon. Guardedly, he watched the people as they came in just before starting time. There were twice as many as he had expected. He surmised that curiosity had brought many of them.

His biggest surprise came when he saw Grumpy Rush and Dett Skeen come in and find a place in the front row. That put Trego's problem right at his fingertips. He had expected Skeen to stay outside and try to shoot him through a window or possibly step inside the church with a gun while he was preaching. Then he realized that there might be somebody else outside to do the shooting while Skeen distracted Trego's attention. Even if Skeen had written the threat, it didn't mean that he'd pull the trigger himself.

Trego's first sermon in Genesis was going to be a real test.

# 5

Trego sat in his chair, half hidden from the crowd by the big pulpit, and waited for the service to begin. Martha Ekhart played the organ in the corner, pumping furiously to generate enough air to send the music over the room. Vona Ekhart led the singing. Trego was surprised at how well she could sing.

Almost before he realized it, the time came for him to step forward and give his sermon. The moment he stood up, the disturbance in the front row began. Trego didn't need to look to locate the source. Dett Skeen and Grumpy Rush were going to create so much diversion that anything Trego said from the pulpit would be completely lost on his audience.

Trego stood behind the pulpit without saying a word. His eyes flashed from one window to another. No one seemed to be outside. Perhaps the two were confident they could totally disrupt the service from the front row. Trego's eyes finally settled on the two in front of him. They talked louder, aiming indirect threats at him. Trego saw Skeen inch around so his gun was within easy grasp.

Trego brought up the gun from his holster, hiding his movements behind the pulpit. Then he slapped it down on the top of the pulpit with a crack that echoed over the room.

"This is a worship service," he said distinctly in the absolute silence that followed. "There will be no interruptions. I have been informed that some people think I am a holy terror with my fists. Let me enlighten you with the fact that I am much better with a gun than with my fists." His eyes bored into Skeen and Rush. "Now fellows, I'm giving you a choice. You can worship peacefully with the rest of us. Or we can have a lesson in gun gospel first and then we'll praise the Lord afterward. Which will it be?"

Grumpy Rush's jaw dropped open until Trego thought he could have shoved his gun down his throat without touching his teeth. Skeen stared at Trego in total disbelief. Trego lifted the gun gently from the pulpit top.

"Your choice, gentlemen."

"We ain't giving no trouble," Rush finally said, scooting down in his seat.

Skeen looked around. "We'll leave," he said.

"No." Trego said sharply. "You'll stay, either willingly or unwillingly; it makes no difference to me. But you won't interrupt the service. If you do, we'll just hold the funeral while we're all here."

Rush was convinced. Skeen's face showed that he wasn't sure how serious Trego was, but he harbored enough doubts that he sank quietly back into his seat.

Trego proceeded with his sermon, sure now that all his trouble was right before him in that front row. It was squelched for the moment. He gave his sermon on brotherly love, using "Love they neighbor as thyself" for his text. It was totally incongruous, he thought, with his gun on the pulpit within inches of his hand. But his audience listened attentively. Everyone was probably afraid not to, he thought. He doubted if Genesis had ever heard a sermon from the point of a gun before.

As soon as the service was over, Rush and Skeen cut a swath through the rest of the congregation getting to the door. Horace Dibble braced against the tide of departing people to shake Trego's hand.

"That was a fine sermon," he said. "Probably the only one Grumpy or Dett ever sat through. It did my soul good to see them there."

"I didn't come here to preach with a gun in my hand, but if that's the way it has to be, I can do it."

"I believe you," Dibble said. "If you need any help, count on me."

"I'll remember that," Trego said. The little bald-headed man seemed to be one of his staunchest supporters.

Tom Ekhart came by then with his family to shake Trego's hand. "That was a lesson this town needed," he said. "I'm referring, of course, to the content of your sermon."

"I doubted if you meant the gun," Trego said with a grin.

"Will you come out for dinner?" Martha Ekhart asked.

Trego turned to her, his eyes catching Vona just behind her mother. Vona acted as bashful as a sixteen year old but he guessed she was at least twenty. "I'll be happy to come," he said. "I'll leave the gun at home."

"Bring it," Tom said. "Just don't eat with it."

Trego turned then to greet the Oyler family. Cal Oyler had a good word to say about the sermon and his wife, Neleda, and daughter, Alvena, congratulated Trego. The Bridgewoods were equally generous with their praise. Web Myrick and his wife reminded Trego that they had made good on their promise to be there. Trego was a little surprised to see Quint and Yonnie Guzek there. He'd heard so much about them that he felt he knew them even if he'd never seen them before.

Quint Guzek was nearing fifty, a small man with graying hair and sharp black eyes that bored into anything he looked at. His wife was almost as tall as her husband but twice as heavy. Trego pushed away the passing thought that she reminded him of a cow that had bloated on damp alfalfa.

Trego got his horse and rode out to Ekhart's as soon as the crowd had left the church. Tom Ekhart had gone on with his family, and Trego didn't intend to be late for dinner.

During dinner, Trego tried to keep his eyes on what he was eating and his mind on the conversation. But he could not ignore Vona. He caught himself searching her out every time he looked up.

"Like to look at the crops?" Tom asked, when dinner was over.

Trego was no farmer, but there was little room for any answer but yes, so he left the house with Tom and they went out beyond the barn where Ekhart had broken the sod and planted some corn. It looked surprisingly good to Trego.

"If we get enough rain, it will make a fine crop," Tom said. "Do you know the blacksmith in town, Furtak? They call him Jumbo."

Trego nodded. "I met him the first night I was in town. Didn't see him at church this morning."

"You're not liable to see him in church — unless it's his own funeral. He's been shining up to Vona. Just thought you'd like to know."

Trego realized that Tom hadn't been blind to his attraction to Vona. "I take it you approve of that?"

"I didn't say," Tom said. "There's more to it than meets the eye. Vona found out I'm suspicious of a lot of people around here, and she took a hand. Can't say that I approve but she does find out a lot more than I can."

Trego frowned. "You suspect Furtak of something?"

"I suspect everybody. Like I told you at Sage Creek, there's something funny going on around here. Strangers just never show up in Genesis except going through on the stage. I think Furtak knows something about that. He's not too bright, just big and strong as a bull. Vona thinks she can find out things from him. I just hope she doesn't become attracted to him. Strange things happen when men and girls get together."

Trego nodded. "From what I've seen of both of them, I can't think of a worse mismatch. Just what do you think is going on, Tom?"

"I wish I knew." Tom picked up a clod of dirt and tossed it carelessly out into the field. "Personally, I don't think that was an accident that killed our former preacher, Oliver Knowles. I think it was murder."

"Why would anybody kill him?"

"He was a lot like you. He had to know what was going on. I think he found out too much. There was no reason for that team to run off the road and over the canyon rim. In fact, I never saw a team that would go over a canyon wall without an awful lot of help."

"Do you suspect the Winchester Gang I've been hearing about?"

"That's as good a guess as any. But who belongs to the Winchester Gang? I suspect Furtak. Your cousin, Pace, suspects Cal Oyler. I can't quite go along with that. Cal's a good churchgoer. He has a fine wife and daughter."

Trego nodded as Tom started slowly back toward the house. "Do you have any idea where I should start looking for my uncle?"

"None at all. Maybe he didn't even come this way. Or maybe he was robbed and left to die like you were except that nobody found him."

"Uncle Luther and I were going to buy a ranch together. Maybe he was coming here to try to buy some land so he and Aunt Ruth could live close to Pace."

"Anything is possible." Ekhart looked at Trego. "The thing that sticks in my craw is that I know of several people who started to Genesis but none of them got here. It doesn't make sense."

Ekhart picked up his pace as a spring wagon turned into the yard. "Yonnie must have heard you were coming for dinner. She'll have plenty of questions."

Trego decided that Tom Ekhart had already told him most of what he knew about this situation that plainly had him puzzled. There hadn't been much that Trego hadn't heard before except his suspicion of Furtak and Vona's involvement with him. In a subtle way, he had warned Trego to go easy where Vona was concerned. He'd do that but he didn't like the idea of leaving Furtak with a clear field. Vona was too good for the blacksmith.

Quint Guzek pulled the team to a halt and Yonnie flounced over the side of the wagon in a surprising show of agility for her size.

"Thought I'd find you here, Preacher," she said. "How do you like it in Genesis?"

"Fine so far," Trego said, reminding himself not to say too much to Yonnie Guzek.

"I liked the way you handled those two hellions. Whipped them yesterday and made them sit there and listen to a sermon on love today. Best two days they ever spent. What do you think they'll do now?"

"Haven't thought about it."

"You'd better or you'll be dead before you know it. Got a wife?"

Trego shook his head. "No."

"Shake a leg, Preacher. We've got some good girls around Genesis. There's one right here at Tom's. Another one in town. And how about the Green girl?"

"I hear she and Roger Sorenson are getting married," Trego said.

"I've heard that, too. There's many a slip between the cup and the lip. You're bigger than that puny Sorenson, Preacher. You can beat him out."

"The missus is in the house," Tom said,

directing Yonnie that way.

Trego silently thanked Tom for sending Yonnie on to the house. They turned to Quint Guzek and the little man who had been riding in the back. Trego learned that he was Oscar Coy, the cook at the ZK ranch. He was in his mid-sixties, at least fifteen years older than Quint Guzek. After the Guzeks had left half an hour later, Tom told Trego that Coy knew all the news of the country but he got it secondhand from Yonnie.

Martha and Vona came outside, Martha fanning the door. "The house is full of words. It needs airing."

Tom chuckled. "Yawn-ie can really rattle the roof with her tongue."

"Does she always tell the truth?" Trego asked.

"Always?" Tom shook his head. "Never. If truth was a bowl of water, she could stretch it till it would flood the Grand Canyon."

Trego thanked the ladies for his dinner, got his horse, and rode back toward town. He stopped for a few minutes to visit with Pace and Katie Holcomb. They'd had no hint that Luther was coming to Genesis. Trego reached town as puzzled as ever.

He spent a restless night, dreaming once that someone was trying to burn his house with him in it. In another dream he saw white-headed Furtak running off with a girl. But it wasn't Vona; it was Alvena Oyler. After that, he didn't sleep again.

He cleaned the house during the morning and looked through some notes for another sermon idea. After eating lunch, he got his horse and rode out of town to the southeast. If there was any clue to what had happened to Luther Holcomb, it surely must be somewhere along the road between Sage Creek and Genesis.

Three hours of riding along the road and into canyons near the road turned up nothing. He reined the horse back toward town. It was then that he saw a rider coming toward him. He recognized Alvena Oyler.

"Going my way?" Trego asked as she pulled up.

"Why not?" She smiled. "I'm ready to head back to town."

"Do you go riding every day?"

"Almost," Alvena said. "You can thank your stars for that. If I hadn't been riding Friday, Horace and I wouldn't have found you tied to that tree."

"Consider my stars dutifully thanked," Trego said.

"Would you come over to our place for supper tomorrow evening?" she asked.

"I'd love to. But are you sure your folks want me?"

"Positive," Alvena said. "Mama told me to ask you if I saw you. I knew you rode out this way after dinner so I came out, hoping I'd meet you."

"That makes me lucky," Trego said. "Maybe you can help me sort out some of the people around here."

"What do you want to know?"

Trego let his horse drop to a walk as they followed the stage road toward town. "What kind of a person is Jumbo Furtak? He didn't come to church yesterday, I noticed."

"He won't, either," Alvena said. "He's no churchgoer. I never saw anyone so strong. He's got muscles like a rock and a head to match."

Trego grinned. "I take it you're not infatuated with Furtak. Horace Dibble seems very nice. I assume you think so, too?"

Alvena was not as quick with an answer this time. "Horace is a good druggist. He and Pa get along pretty well. They are both businessmen. He's a good friend of the family but not special."

"I thought maybe he was," Trego said.

"I didn't invite him to ride with me Friday," Alvena said quickly. "He saw me leave town and rode out to catch up with

71

me. I guess it was lucky he did. He helped cut you down. Horace thinks he has a special interest in me." Color crept up in her cheeks. "Why, he's older than Pa!"

"That doesn't dim some men's interest."

"That's obvious," Alvena admitted. "I like men more my age."

Trego saw where this was leading, and he wasn't sure he was quite ready for that. He turned the conversation to another man in town. "The deputy sheriff, Petrauk, didn't seem too excited about having a new preacher in town."

"Fred is a good deputy so far as I know," Alvena said. "I don't have any use for those helpers of his, Grumpy and Dett."

"Can't say that I'm really in love with them, either," Trego said.

"Oh, yes," Alvena added, "Buck Adalbert will be at supper tomorrow night, too. He drives the stage to Sage Creek and back, then Jason Cobb takes it on to Hawk's Nest and back. They stay here in Genesis between trips. You'll like him, I think."

"What do you know about the Bridge-woods?"

"I like them," Alvena said quickly. "They have helped the settlers, and it's the settlers that keep our store going."

Shadows started to creep down into the

canyons as the sun sank toward the horizon. Trego suddenly caught a movement at the rim of the canyon to his right. He wheeled that way, his hand dropping automatically to his gun. The canyon rim was lifeless.

Alvena touched his arm. "What's wrong?"

"I'm not sure anything is." Trego didn't take his eyes off the spot where he'd caught that movement. "I just don't feel like taking chances."

He caught a flick of movement again a little more to his right. Again it disappeared instantly. Instinct told him that he was just a whisper away from the grave.

# 6

Trego lifted his gun out of the holster, his eyes searching the rim of the canyon. He was sure he had seen the head of a man in two different places, so there had to be at least two men out there. Suddenly Alvena rode between him and the canyon rim. He hadn't noticed her coming around from his other side.

"Move back," he said softly. "If they're after me, they might hit you."

"They won't shoot at a woman," she said firmly. "If somebody is after you, there will probably be more than one. You can't whip them all." She looked back toward the canyon rim. Except for the fear in her face, Trego would have thought she was as calm as if she were at a Sunday picnic.

"A bushwhacker isn't always careful who he shoots," Trego said, reaching for the reins of her horse.

She pulled them out of his reach. "They

won't shoot me. We lost one preacher. I don't propose to lose another one if I can help it."

They moved on up the road, Alvena keeping her pace with Trego. Trego tried to see around her to the canyon rim. He was sure he saw a head pop up once more, but no shots were fired. Fifty yards ahead, the road cut away from the canyon. They were rapidly getting out of range of anyone hiding behind the rim. But there was still a prickly feeling at the base of Trego's scalp. He'd been in the jaws of an ambush. Just because Alvena had foiled this one didn't mean there wouldn't be another one. He'd have to watch where he went and keep an eye on his back trail.

"You shouldn't have done that," Trego said when they were safely away from the canyon rim. "I might as well settle these things as they come up."

Alvena shook her head. "They're calling you The Holy Terror. But not even a holy terror can survive a shot in the back."

"I just don't like to run from a fight," Trego growled, realizing how many times that very attitude had gotten him into trouble.

"An ambush is not a fight." she said. She smiled now that the danger was past. "Anyway, I wasn't going to be cheated out of a guest I had already invited to supper." She put her horse into a lope and Trego nudged his horse out of a walk to keep up.

They put their horses in the barn and Trego walked Alvena home before returning to the parsonage. Anger surged through him as he saw the interior of his house. Papers were scattered over the back room that he'd selected for his study and a chair was upset, testifying to the haste of the intruders. Trego picked up the papers slowly, wondering what anybody could be looking for in the parsonage. He certainly didn't have anything worth stealing. Was it something that the previous minister had left? There was nothing in the scattered papers to give him a clue.

That was still on his mind as he got his horse the next morning and headed out on the road back to Sage Creek. Today he was determined to settle in his own mind whether or not Luther Holcomb had tried to get to Genesis.

There were a few small ranches and farms along the road between the canyons several miles back toward Sage Creek. If Luther had come this way, one of those settlers ought to remember seeing him. At the first stage stop, he asked. But the man admitted that he didn't pay any attention to anything except his horses. A short distance beyond the stage station, he came to a ranch. Although it was closer to Genesis than Sage Creek, it claimed Sage Creek as its home address. The man Trego talked to couldn't remember that anyone answering Luther's description had come by. But he admitted that he didn't see everybody who went up the road. Most of his working hours were spent miles from the road.

The next place Trego reached was a small farm right along the road. The man here, a stoop-shouldered stringbean of a figure, looking more like a ghost than a living human, listened as Trego described Luther. He nodded. He had seen such a man two or three weeks ago. He had stopped for a drink of water.

Trego rode back toward Genesis, convinced that Luther Holcomb had come toward Genesis. Somewhere between that farm and town, something had happened to him.

The sun was only half way down the western sky when Trego came in sight of Genesis. There was time to ride across Ash Creek Canyon to Pace's and tell him what he'd learned. Swinging across to the road that ran out to the homesteads, he dropped

77

down into Ash Creek Canyon and across the little stream, through the trees that bordered it, and up the far slope covered with bunch grass.

Pace was in the field, but he came to the house when he saw Trego. Tying his team by the barn, he came into the house and got a long drink of water.

"Find out anything?" he asked, turning to Trego.

"Found a farmer out south who remembers seeing Uncle Luther about two or three weeks ago. He stopped there to get a drink. Something must have happened between there and Genesis."

"Wish we could find out what," Pace said.

Trego headed back to town, wrestling with this puzzle. Luther was missing, and there was no communication between Pace and his mother. He could understand a letter now and then getting lost. But an explanation was called for when all letters between here and Sage Creek disappeared.

Trego got back to town in time to wash up and change clothes before time to go to Oyler's for supper. He was met at the door of the house behind Oyler's store by Alvena, who obviously had been watching for him.

"I was afraid you might forget," she said. "I didn't see you all day."

"I've been out roaming around," Trego said. Then he grinned. "I'm not liable to forget an invitation to supper. A bachelor soon gets tired of his own cooking."

Alvena led him into the living room where Cal Oyler was sitting with a tall thin man with sad blue eyes and stringy brown hair that fell over his eyes when he shifted his head. A long drooping mustache reached down to his chin and then curled back up in little circles.

"This is Buck Adalbert," Alvena said. "Buck, this is our new preacher, Sam Trego."

Adalbert got up, tossing his head to get the long hair out of his eyes. He reached a hand to Trego. Trego found his grip something less than powerful.

"Always glad to meet a preacher," Adalbert said. He grinned, showing two broken teeth in the front of his mouth. "If you ride the stage, you'll sure cramp my style with the team."

"Maybe your teams have just been taught the wrong language," Trego said.

While the two women finished the supper, Trego sat with Cal Oyler and Adalbert. He didn't know what they had been talking about but he was sure that his arrival had sidetracked the subject. He wondered how often his appearance had changed the course of a conversation. That was one of the disadvantages of his calling. He failed to learn a lot of things he'd like to know and might have learned if he hadn't been wearing the tag of Preacher.

"I've heard the Winchester Gang mentioned two or three times since I came here," Trego interjected into a pause in the conversation. "Know anything about them?"

Cal Oyler's face was grim. "You'll hear about that gang off and on," he said.

"Does the gang hide out in the canyons around here?"

Oyler nodded. "No doubt about it. Somebody in that gang obviously doesn't like preachers, either."

"How do you know that?" Trego asked.

"From things that have been said — and done."

"Do you blame them for Oliver Knowles' death?"

Trego looked from Oyler to Adalbert. They seemed to know something, but were reluctant to part with the knowledge.

"I wouldn't say that right out," Oyler said when Adalbert held his silence. "A couple of warning notes were found at the parsonage. They were almost certainly from the

Winchester Gang. Knowles' death was marked down as an accident, but it seems odd that a team of well-broke horses would just run over a canyon rim."

That was the second time Trego had heard that. By now he was convinced that Knowles had been murdered. The question was, why? It seemed unreasonable that anybody would just hate preachers because they were preachers. Had Knowles been something else? Had he stumbled onto their hideout or their identities?

"Have you seen any of the gang?" Trego asked.

"Not so we can recognize them," Adalbert said, speaking up for the first time. "They've held up my stage a couple of times. But they always wear masks."

"I've never seen any of them so far as I know," Cal Oyler added. "But there is no doubt the gang is in this country. They've held up stagecoaches, robbed and even killed people."

Neleda Oyler called into the room that supper was ready. The subject of the Winchester Gang was dropped. Trego went in to supper, turning over what little he had learned. Hidden in that vague information was a warning to him. The Winchester Gang seemed to hate preachers. Trego was convinced that they'd have a good reason for hating him if they found out what he was really here for. It seemed reasonable that the Winchester Gang was to blame for the disappearance of Luther Holcomb. Likely the motive was simply robbery, but what had happened to Luther?

Trego put it from his mind when he saw the loaded table. It had been a long time since he'd sat down to a meal like that. There was steak and prairie chicken. Either one would have been a feast for Trego. Mashed potatoes and gravy, string beans, canned peaches, and a dried apple pie all caught his eye as his hungry glance swept over the table.

Talk died down as they all paid full homage to the meal. Twenty minutes later, each one pushed his chair back as if that was as much as his remaining energy could do. Neleda and Alvena got up and started clearing the food off the table. It seemed a shame to Trego to see so much food that couldn't be eaten.

Within a few minutes the table was clear. Then Alvena came in and motioned to Trego. "Want to see the town before it gets dark?" she asked.

Trego got up. He didn't think Cal Oyler or Adalbert would regret seeing him go.

They seemed to have a lot in common and he was sure that when he had arrived, he had interrupted a conversation that they'd like to continue.

"I'd like that," Trego said, "if the others will excuse me."

"Go ahead," Adalbert said. "You'd be a fool to pass up a chance to walk over town with a pretty girl."

"Wonderful meal," Trego said as he left the house with Alvena. "How did you escape washing dishes?"

"Mama said she'd do them if I'd show you the town. We want you to like it here. We need a preacher."

"I like it, all right," he said. "I just seem to run afoul of the wrong people. What do you know about the Winchester Gang?"

"Very little," she admitted. "Mostly just what Pa tells us. He hears about everything that goes on, being a storekeeper and also postmaster."

As they moved slowly toward the south end of town, they met Dibble out with his dog returning from a tour of the town. Trego was sure that was jealousy on his little round face as he watched them go by. But he answered courteously when Trego spoke to him.

"There's a lonely man," Alvena said when

Dibble had gone on. "Why aren't you married?"

Trego grinned. "Think I'll end up lonely like him? Maybe I will. Who knows? A preacher doesn't make enough money to support a wife, you know."

"That doesn't keep most preachers from getting married," Alvena said.

Trego could almost feel himself being maneuvered into a corner. Maybe Alvena didn't realize where the conversation was going, but he did and he changed the subject quickly to talk about Adalbert and the stage holdups. But Alvena knew no more about the holdups than what Adalbert had told him.

After touring the town, which didn't take long, Trego walked Alvena home, then returned to the parsonage. He had gotten an idea, born when Alvena had mentioned how her father learned many things as storekeeper and postmaster. He had to test that idea.

Morning found him back in the saddle headed out to Pace Holcomb's again. He asked Pace to write a letter to his mother in Sage Creek, and he would take it to town and mail it at the post office.

"I've been doing that since we moved

here," Pace said, "and apparently none of my letters of the last month have gone through."

"That's just the point," Trego said. "Those letters go astray somewhere. I have an idea how I might find out where. If I do, then maybe I'll be a little closer to learning where Uncle Luther and his money went."

Pace agreed. "I'll do anything to find out that." He sat down and scribbled a short note to his mother, put it in an envelope, and sealed it.

"I'll stamp it in town and mail it," Trego said.

He took the letter and rode back to town. Leaving his horse at the livery, he walked up the street to Oyler's store. There was no one in the store but Cal Oyler. Trego bought a stamp at the little square room set aside for the post office in the back of the store. Sticking the stamp to the letter, he handed it to Cal and watched him toss it in with a dozen or so other letters to go out when the stage came through.

Trego went outside. He knew that the stage was due within the hour. Moving along the side of the store until he reached the window that let light into the post office corner, he paused, dipping his head to see what Oyler was doing.

It was ten minutes before Oyler came back to the post office. Then he picked up the box of letters to go out and began sorting and postmarking them. Cautiously, Trego spied on him. He saw him take one letter out of the pile and lay it aside while he worked on the others. When Trego saw what Cal Oyler did with that letter, he'd have his suspicions confirmed or destroyed. He couldn't be sure that was Pace's letter to Ruth. But if Oyler threw it away, Trego would find out whose letter it was, if he had to break into the post office to do it.

Suddenly he felt a terrific burn across his shoulders. Wheeling, he saw Grumpy Rush and Dett Skeen near the front of the store. Grumpy had a long bull whip in his hand. He had just laid the lash across Trego's shoulders and was drawing it back for another crack.

# 7

A dozen things flashed through Trego's mind as he saw the whip being drawn back for another strike at him. If he would turn and run, he might be out of range of the whip before it could reach him again. But Trego's immediate reaction was to get to the whip wielder and tear him to pieces. There was a stubbornness in him that fought against running from anything but certain death.

His eyes flashed over the two men. Grumpy was standing in front of Skeen. That apparently was Skeen's strategy whenever there was any danger. Trego's eyes swept over the two men for guns. Skeen, at least, usually had a gun. But not today. They must have been in Oyler's store and seen him through a window. Unarmed, they had grabbed one of the whips that Oyler had on display and ran around here.

The lash was coming forward again,

propelled by all the strength that Grumpy Rush had. Trego dodged at the last instant, and the lash whistled past him. Rush jerked the lash back and cocked his arm to strike again. He had none of the talent of a mule-skinner; he couldn't maneuver that long lash with any real accuracy. This time Trego timed his lunge and grabbed at the lash as it came forward. He caught it two feet from the end. The tail of the lash wrapped itself around Trego's neck, burning like fire. But he held on and jerked.

Rush braced himself, cursing wickedly. Skeen grabbed hold of the whip handle, too, and tugged against Trego's strength. Trego was stout, but he was not strong enough to jerk the whip away from both men. He suddenly leaped forward, letting the whip go slack. Both Rush and Skeen, pulling with heels dug into the ground, flopped on their backs.

Trego dashed forward, getting a grip on the whip close to the handle. With a twisting jerk, he tore it from Rush's grasp. Skeen had let go of the whip when he was falling, trying to get out of the way of Grumpy coming down on top of him.

Trego got a solid grip on the whip handle as the two men scrambled wildly to their feet. He let them get a start toward the corner of the store, then he brought the whip around with all the force he had. He had none of the finesse of a muleskinner, either, but he had power.

Rush's long legs carried him past Skeen, and the little man caught the brunt of Trego's whip. He screamed like a dying cougar, then charged around the corner in Rush's wake. If Trego hadn't been hurting from the lash across his own back or the burn on his neck, he could have enjoyed Skeen's discomfort. Those two had certainly given him a full quota of miserable moments.

Trego took the whip back into the store and handed it to Oyler who was in the front part of the building now. He explained that Rush and Skeen had apparently taken it from the store to use on him. Oyler acted as though he doubted Trego's story, but he said nothing and jammed the whip back into the keg where the other whips were on display, butts in the keg, lashes trailing to the floor.

Trego glanced at the post office in the corner. He knew that by now that letter was either in the mail pouch ready to go out on the stage or else destroyed. He could never find it, so he had nothing but his suspicion that Oyler had taken out Pace's letter.

At the parsonage Trego got himself an early lunch although he didn't feel much like eating. He found some salve and spread it as best he could on his back and neck. His shirt had been cut by the whip lash and there was blood on the back. After putting on a clean shirt, he went down to the barn and got his horse.

Trego had reached the conclusion that Luther Holcomb was dead. Maybe someone had known he was carrying that money and had robbed him, killing him so there would be no witness. Remembering how Luther always dressed, it wasn't likely that a robber would hold him up unless he had definite knowledge that Luther was carrying a lot of money. Luther Holcomb always dressed like the dirt farmer he was. He had a special sky-blue sweater that he wore when he was dressing up for town or church. It was the only concession he made to social etiquette. Certainly his dress would not suggest wealth.

So today Trego was looking for a shallow grave somewhere near the road between Sage Creek and Genesis. When he reached the place where he had been held up, he turned into the ravine leading down into the canyon. It was a perfect place for an ambush, so he suspected that Luther might have been waylaid here, too.

He let his horse pick its way down the steep incline to the level where an occasional tree grew. Farther down, the small gully where water ran during rains was lined with trees. A good meadow of grass dotted here and there with trees filled the floor of the canyon. It was a narrow canyon, more suited for a robber's hideout than farming or even grazing.

Trego searched carefully among the cottonwood and ash trees. There were a few stunted and dead willow trees, testifying to wetter seasons in the past that had nurtured the willows. There the ground was rocky, Trego hurried on. Anyone burying a body would pick a spot where the ground was soft.

He was passing a clump of small cottonwood trees, still looking for disturbed ground, when his eye caught a glimpse of something that looked like a boot back in the trees. He reined up quickly. Dismounting, he walked into the trees. He saw the sole of the boot again, toe pointed toward the sky. Moving past one of the small trees, he saw the other boot beside it.

His first thought was that he had found Luther. But then he realized that those boots did not belong to Luther. He always wore work shoes. Pushing farther into the trees, he saw the chalk rocks and a little dirt covering the body. It had been a very hasty and careless job. He wouldn't even call it a burial.

He pushed a rock carefully to one side to get a look at the face. It was a young man and he hadn't been here very long, probably no longer than a day.

Turning back to his horse, he swung into the saddle and put his horse up the steep slope to the road. This was something for the deputy sheriff to look into. He wondered if this was another case of robbery and murder. He had been thinking that Luther's disappearance might be an isolated case. This suggested that it might not be.

In Genesis, he reined up in front of the deputy sheriff's office next to the boarding-house. Dismounting, he hurried inside but the office was empty. He thought of the two men who had quit Guzek's ranch to work for Petrauk, Grumpy Rush and Dett Skeen. They spent a lot of time in the back room of Dibble's drugstore, the only recreation parlor and bar in town. Maybe Petrauk was there, too.

He left his horse at the hitchrack in front of the deputy's office and strode up the street. At the town hall, he crossed the street to Dibble's. The big white bulldog met him at the door. Trego gave him a long look. If that dog was half as vicious as he looked, Dibble wouldn't have any customers.

The dog turned to follow Trego with his baleful gaze as he went to the counter. "Is Petrauk in the back?" Trego asked the druggist.

Dibble nodded. "He went in not ten minutes ago."

Trego went through the back door. He saw Skeen first, then he spotted Rush and Petrauk across the table from him. Fear and suspicion sharpened Skeen's eyes. Rush pushed his chair back with a squeak.

Trego pretended to ignore the two as he concentrated on the deputy sheriff. But he was aware of every move they made.

"I found a body out in the canyons," Trego announced. "I figure you ought to take a look."

"Who did you kill?" Petrauk asked acidly.

Trego's eyes hardened and he shot a look at Skeen. "The nearest I came to killing anyone was to take a little hide off a sidewinder's back."

Skeen scowled but he said nothing. Petrauk glared at Trego then started toward the door, jerking his thumb at the other two. They got up to follow him.

"I figure we can do whatever has to be done," Trego said, glaring at the two tagging after Petrauk.

"You've done your duty," Petrauk said. "You've reported it. I'll bring in the body."

Trego suspected that if Petrauk went out there alone or with his two helpers, nobody would ever see that body again. It would be buried deep and far away where no one would find it.

"You don't know where it is," he said. "I'll go along and show you."

"You can tell me which canyon it's in," Petrauk said.

"I don't know the names of these canyons like you do. I'll just go along."

Petrauk hesitated. This wasn't to his liking. He looked back at Skeen and Rush. Trego shook his head.

"We don't need them."

The two stopped and Petrauk went on into the main room with Trego. They got a wagon from the livery barn and drove out on the road toward Sage Creek. At the dip where it crossed the swale leading to the canyon, Trego directed Petrauk off the road into the canyon, then toward the little grove of cottonwoods.

Petrauk denied knowing the dead man but Trego didn't believe him. They put the body in the wagon and hauled it back to town. Petrauk suggested they bury the body immediately in the cemetery just outside town. Trego insisted on checking with people to see if anybody could identify the dead man. He must have had some reason for coming into this country. Petrauk finally agreed to ride out and tell the Holcombs, Ekharts, and Myricks.

Trego watched him go, then he rode to the east. The Greens lived out this way. He suspected that Petrauk knew more about the dead man than he was telling. Since he was so willing to ride southwest of town to tell the people there, maybe it was a relative of somebody to the east.

By the time Trego got back with Bill Green, Pace Holcomb and Tom Ekhart were already in town. It was Green who recognized the man.

"That's my nephew, Jim, my brother's boy. I didn't know he was coming here till the wedding."

For the moment, Trego had forgotten Amy Green's wedding to Roger Sorenson, the livery man. He was to perform that wedding in just a few days.

"Did he have any money on him?" Green asked.

Trego shook his head. "I saw Petrauk

search him. Nothing in his pockets."

"That's understandable," Green said. "He seldom carried much money."

"Robbery is a good possibility as a motive," Trego said. "We need to bury him right away."

"His mother should be here," Bill Green said. "His father is dead, but she would come if possible."

"We can't wait that long," Trego said. "We'll have the burial today. Then we can have a memorial service for him Sunday. His mother could be here then."

Trego conducted the funeral at sundown and Green sent a hired man to tell his sister-in-law to come for the memorial service on Sunday. Trego was especially eager to see her and ask some questions. He was beginning to see a pattern and he needed verification of his suspicions.

Laura Green arrived on Saturday. Trego met the stage when she came in. Bill Green was there, too. After expressing his sympathy, Trego asked Mrs. Green a question. "Did your son bring any money with him when he came?"

"I didn't even know he was coming," she said. "But I found out at the bank when I went to get money for this trip that he had withdrawn four thousand dollars the day he left, almost all we had. Was it found?"

Trego shook his head. "There was no money on him. Robbery was probably the motive for his murder."

Another idea was whirling through Trego's mind. At last, it was beginning to make sense to him. He was sure that Luther Holcomb was dead and very likely his death was similar to that of Jim Green's. Both had been carrying about all the money they had. The question was why they had brought that money here.

To Trego, it sounded like an extortion plot. But what kind of extortion? Kidnapping crossed his mind. However, nobody here at Genesis had been kidnapped. Then suddenly it hit him. Who had to know there had been no kidnapping? The folks outside these canyons like Ruth Holcomb and Laura Green didn't even know their relatives had come to Genesis. And the people here in Genesis didn't know their relatives were coming, certainly not to ransom them. The relatives with the money never got here alive.

Trego realized that was just a wild theory. He wouldn't dare tell anybody or they'd think he was crazy.

He talked to Laura Green again Saturday evening. "Did your son get a letter just before he came over here?"

She thought for a moment. "Why, yes, I think he did. I didn't see it. I don't read his mail. But I can't see what that could have to do with what happened."

"Do you know where the letter came from?"

"No. He had lots of friends. I remember thinking that his cousin, Amy, was probably sending him a personal invitation to her wedding here in Genesis."

It was nothing definite, but Trego felt he had one of the missing links. That letter might have been like the one Luther Holcomb received. "Will you be staying for Amy's wedding now that you're here?"

"Maybe," she said. "Under the circumstances, it's hard to plan ahead."

"You don't think Amy will want to postpone the wedding?"

"I wouldn't think of letting her do it," Laura Green said quickly. "Putting off the wedding won't help Jim any. We have to go on living."

Trego went on home after getting everything at the church ready for the special services tomorrow morning. That was when he found the note on the door.

"You're getting too nosey. Take care. A lot of accidents happen around Genesis."

The note was unsigned. But then nobody in his right mind would sign that. He thought of what his uncle had said once. A rattler never rattles more than twice before he strikes. Trego wasn't sure how true that was, but he wouldn't question the accuracy in regard to this note.

## 8

The Sunday service went off smoothly. Trego was uneasy, watching every window and the door, even keeping an eye on people in the congregation. The people he had mentally tabbed as the ones to watch were not in evidence. Grumpy Rush and Dett Skeen headed the list. Fred Petrauk, the deputy, was another one whose animosity was obvious. And he was sure Jumbo Furtak would bear watching. He wasn't sure how much deeper into the town citizens he'd have to dip to gather up all the ones who might strike at him.

Horace Dibble walked his dog as usual just at sundown that evening and as he came by the parsonage, he saw Trego at the door and came over. Trego welcomed one of the few men who was very friendly toward him.

"That was a nice service for the Green boy," Dibble said. "You're proving to be a good preacher."

"What were you expecting?" Trego asked.

Dibble shrugged. "When you bring in a total stranger, you never know what to expect. And when we had to rescue you from that tree down in the canyon, it raised a real question. Apparently somebody had already decided that you should not preach for us."

"How do you feel about it?" Trego asked.

Dibble laughed. "Well, you know how I feel. I'm in your corner all the way."

Trego brought out the note he'd found on the door last night. "Have any idea who might have written that?" he asked.

The druggist examined the note carefully. "I'd say it was Skeen or Rush except I don't think either one can write that well. It might have been Fred Petrauk. I've noticed he doesn't seem to cotton to you."

"I've been aware of that," Trego said.

"I wouldn't worry about it," Dibble said. "But I wouldn't push my luck, either. There are too many people with itchy fingers. Remember what happened to the preacher before you."

"I'm not forgetting," Trego said.

"Well, good night," Dibble said as he followed his dog on down the street. "Sleep well."

Trego wasn't too sure how well he'd sleep. The wedding of Amy Green to Roger Sorenson was tomorrow evening at the church. He had done many of the things expected of a minister and, though he had the authority to marry people, he had never actually performed a ceremony before. It would be easier if he didn't have to keep an eye open for trouble all the time.

By the middle of the forenoon the next day, Alvena Oyler was at the church to start decorating for the wedding. Within half an hour she was joined by Vona Ekhart and Uldine Myrick. The Myricks were special friends of the Greens, Trego had been told.

He stayed around for a short while until he saw that he wasn't going to be needed. The three young women had all the ideas and help they needed. He got an early dinner at the parsonage then got his horse and rode out to the south. Somewhere out here, he'd find more of the secret. He had to do some thinking but while he was doing it, he could look again for his uncle's grave. He was convinced that Luther had been killed out here somewhere near where he'd found the body of Jim Green.

Finding Luther's grave would not really solve anything for Trego. He was sure he already had discovered the real plot behind the murders. He had to find the seven thousand dollars that Luther had brought with him. To do that, he must find the ring leader of this gang of killers.

He reined his horse off the stage road and down into the canyon where he had found Jim Green. He expected to find more graves down here somewhere near that same spot. From the place where he had found the body a few days ago, he moved on, searching every open spot among the trees and out in the meadow for freshly turned ground.

He hadn't gone far in his systematic search when he felt a sudden jerk on his sleeve followed almost instantly by the report of a rifle. Trego dived out of the saddle almost as if the bullet had knocked him out. Hanging on to the reins of his horse, he moved back a few feet into the trees, pulling the horse after him.

Across the saddle, he searched the area where he thought the gunman must be hidden. Several chunks of chalk rock had tumbled down from the canyon rim and rolled out a few feet from the steep slope. It was the only hiding place Trego could see.

His first reaction was to go after whoever had taken that shot at him. But the rock pile was out in the open. The gunman had a view in all directions, and anybody who tried to get to him would have to expose himself.

Pulling his horse farther back into the trees, he got out of sight of the rocks. He mounted his horse and put him back up the canyon through the trees along the creek bed, finally turning toward the stage road. It went against his nature to leave that shot unanswered but he had too much to lose and too little to gain by pressing his luck.

He turned his mind to the wedding tonight as he neared town. He expected most of the neighborhood to be there since everyone was invited. The wedding was set for sundown.

A half hour before sunset, the church was almost full. Trego was amazed at what the three young women had done to the church in the time he'd been gone. Colored paper streamers were tacked along the walls, even weaving across the windows. Flowers, many of them freshly picked from the prairies, decorated the front of the church.

Trego reviewed the book his father had given him while he was still at school. In it, he found a variety of ceremonies for church weddings. All were so similar that he simply chose one that pleased him and seemed to fit the situation.

The wedding went along without a hitch. Still Trego was relieved when the final "I do" had been said and he could pronounce the couple man and wife. As the newly married pair went back down the aisle of the church, Trego had a chance to look around to see just who was here. About the only ones missing so far as he could see were Fred Petrauk and his two helpers, Rush and Skeen. Every businessman in town was here, including the blacksmith, Jumbo Furtak.

The festivities were scheduled to switch to the town hall, up the street just across from Dibble's drugstore. Trego went by the parsonage to change to more comfortable clothes for the big party that was planned.

As he went inside, his eye caught sight of the paper on the table. He didn't recall leaving any paper on the table. He picked it up. There were just five words scrawled on it. "Stay out of the canyons."

If there had been any doubt in his mind that he was getting close to something, it was gone now. It wasn't a very smart man who had left that note here. By now, they should know that warnings only whetted Trego's interest and whatever they warned against was liable to be what he would do.

The party was getting under way by the

time Trego got to the town hall. There was punch and cake for all, but Trego saw within half an hour that somebody was finding something stronger than fruit punch to drink. The worst offender was Jumbo Furtak. He was normally a very quiet man, never saying anything except in answer to a question. He was roaming around the room now, talking in a voice as big as his body.

Somebody had brought a fiddle and when the music began, the center of the floor cleared for the dancers. Trego wasn't much of a dancer so he became a spectator, which seemed to be what was expected of the preacher.

As the dancers began whirling around the floor, Trego made another discovery. Fred Petrauk had arrived. Trego guessed that more whiskey had arrived with him because he was already slightly wobbly on his feet.

Alvena found a chair beside Trego and talked with him during one dance. When Dibble came by and claimed her for the next dance, Vona Ekhart slid into the chair Alvena had vacated.

"Are you enjoying yourself, Reverend?" Vona asked.

"Sure," Trego said. "But I won't be if you keep calling me Reverend. I don't like that title. I don't feel so reverent some of the time."

Vona giggled. "Like the time you cracked Grumpy's and Dett's heads together?"

Trego grinned. "That wasn't exactly what you'd expect from a reverent man, is it?"

"If he lives in Genesis, I think maybe it is," Vona said. "A preacher has to survive in this world before he can preach about the next."

Trego was enjoying his visit with Vona when the music stopped. He considered himself lucky. He'd had the pleasure of the company of two of the prettiest girls at the party and he hadn't even had to struggle through the steps out on the floor.

Furtak came by and caught Vona's hand. "Come on," he roared. "Let's dance."

Vona was jerked to her feet. "I don't think so, Jumbo," she said softly.

"You're my girl," Furtak snapped. "You're going to dance with me."

Vona's jaw set. "No," she said. "You've been drinking."

"Not so that you can notice it," Furtak growled, not letting go of Vona's hand. "Come on." He jerked her off her feet in a big leap toward the center of the floor.

Trego half rose from his chair. This was none of his business. But he couldn't remember when he hadn't responded to a situation like that. He knew he was supposed to conduct himself like a preacher here. Although he wouldn't admit it to anybody else that Vona was something special to him, he would admit it to himself. She was Jumbo Furtak's girl; at least, that was the impression Trego had been given. Right now, she wasn't happy about being dragged out on the floor.

Trego shot a look at Tom Ekhart. Tom was scowling. He didn't like it but he wasn't about to tangle with Furtak. Furtak was huge, not quite as tall as Trego but at least thirty pounds heavier. His strength had never really been tested in the few fights he'd had here at Genesis. Not even Grumpy Rush dared cross Furtak.

Furtak gave Vona another tug to the center of the floor, then turned to the fiddle player and roared, "Let's have some music."

Trego left his chair. "I think not," he said sharply. "Vona doesn't want to dance."

Furtak turned on Trego, still gripping Vona's hand. "Just back off, Preacher," Furtak growled. "She's my girl."

"She's not your slave. Let her go."

Furtak gave Vona a shove that almost sent her sprawling, then charged toward Trego. Trego had expected it. He'd been in many fights like this but never while posing as a preacher. He sidestepped the charge and smashed a fist at Furtak as he went past. Furtak was a brawler like almost every big man Trego had fought. They liked to get it close where their superior strength and weight could make the difference. Trego could hold his own in such a battle, but he took some severe punishment whenever he did.

Furtak came after Trego with the confidence of a grizzly bear. He had never seen the man he couldn't whip with his bare fists. Trego was almost in the same category. Within a minute, those watching knew they were in for a classic battle. Trego heard Vona calling on Petrauk to stop the fight.

"Not on your life," Petrauk yelled. "I've been wanting to see the preacher put in his place. Jumbo will do it."

Obviously, the only thing in Furtak's mind was to get in close and crush his opponent. Trego could box, and now he used all the skill he had learned. He sidestepped, slashing Furtak on the mouth and nose until the blacksmith's shirt front was splattered with blood. Still Trego hadn't let Furtak do more than graze him with a fist now and then. Furtak began to puff like a wind-broken horse. His work in the blacksmith shop hadn't conditioned him for this much sustained effort.

When Trego sensed that Furtak had lost much of his steam, he stood his ground in front of one of Furtak's charges and traded blows with him. His first shot was to his already mashed nose. Furtak howled, but kept coming in. Trego had guessed right. The blacksmith's blows had lost much of their lethal power. Trego took some hard jolts while he handed out his own brand of lethal punishment. The fight finally ended when Furtak's legs began to buckle and he went down on his knees as if he were worshipping Trego. Trego stepped out of the way and the huge man toppled over on his face.

There was a hush in the hall before sound exploded. Trego heard the cheers and realized that most of the people here were delighted to see Furtak beaten. He felt a nudge from the side and looked around to see Fred Petrauk. His hand was on the butt of his gun.

"I'm arresting you for trying to kill a man," Petrauk hissed.

The banker, Ivan Bridgewood, stepped up behind Petrauk, his hand in his coat pocket. "You do, Fred, and you're a dead man. That was a fair fight."

Petrauk wilted like an uprooted sunflower. Trego looked at Bridgewood. There was no mistaking the outline of the snub-nosed derringer in the banker's coat pocket.

"The party's over," Bill Green shouted. "But I say it's been a good one."

A chorus of approval greeted that statement, then people began filing out the front door. Trego went that way, too, beginning to feel the bruises that Furtak had inflicted near the end of the fight.

"Come to our place and let me doctor those bruises," Alvena invited.

Her father caught her arm. "We can't afford to have a brawler like that in our house," he hissed.

"All right," Alvena said spiritedly. "Then I'll go to his place and doctor him." She turned to Trego. "I'll be over as soon as I get the medicine."

Trego nodded, too surprised to either agree or disagree. Alvena was a very strong-willed girl, he saw. As he left the hall, Vona caught up with him and thanked him for rescuing her, but she made no offer to give him any aid. Not that he really needed it, he admitted, but it was nice to have it offered.

It took Alvena only a few minutes to rub salve on the one bruise where the skin was broken and liniment on the other bruises. But she stayed at the parsonage for almost an hour.

"I appreciate your help, Alvena," Trego said finally. "But for the good of your reputation, you'd better get on home."

"If I'm not safe in the preacher's house, where am I safe?"

"Good question," Trego said. "But that's not the way some people will look at it and you know it."

Almost reluctantly she got up and headed for home. For the last half hour, Trego had expected Cal Oyler to come down here to get her.

After she was gone, he turned in. He was sore all over. He had fought for one girl and another one had doctored his battle wounds. He was confused.

Trego was sore the next morning, but he refused to let it show. After breakfast, he got his horse and rode out of town. He noticed that the blacksmith shop had not opened for the day.

He thought of last night and wondered if he had been too puritanical in sending Alvena home. Probably nobody had taken any notice of the fact that she had come to his house or how long she stayed.

He rode in to Ekhart's to discuss that shot

someone had taken at him yesterday. Vona was in the yard when he rode up and dismounted. He saw none of the welcome in her eyes that he had expected.

"Did Alvena spend the whole night with you last night?" she asked acidly.

# 9

Trego stared at Vona. There was no mistaking the accusation in her face or words. Anger surged through him.

"Not that it's any of your business," he snapped, "but she didn't. She might have been good company."

"I'm sure she would have been," Vona said caustically. "I'll bet you thought of it, too."

Anger was growing in Trego. Then it struck him that Vona should not have known that Alvena came to his house.

"How did you find out she was at my place?" he demanded.

"Quint and Yonnie Guzek were at the party. Or don't you remember?"

Trego nodded. "Sure, I remember. Your pa said that Yonnie could stretch the truth like a land speculator."

"Maybe," Vona said. "But she didn't miss it when she said Alvena went to your place."

"No," Trego admitted. "She came to my

place to rub liniment on my bruises. But Yonnie didn't tell you that she went right back home again."

Tom Ekhart came into the yard. "Did you find out anything more about your uncle?"

Trego shook his head, turning his back on Vona who appeared willing to carry on the argument a little longer. "I think I may be getting close. Somebody took a shot at me yesterday when I was in the canyons southeast of town. What do you know about that country over there?"

"Not much," Tom said. "It would be a good hiding place for outlaws. Maybe you bumped into the hideout of the Winchester Gang."

"I thought of that. I'm going back today and see if someone runs me out again."

"You be careful," Tom said. "We don't want to lose another preacher."

Trego nodded and swung back into the saddle. He had thought he'd stay a while, but the frigid reception Vona had given him had killed that desire. He glanced at her now, but she didn't even voice any concern about his safety. She was obviously debating whether to believe him or Yonnie Guzek. If she decided to believe Yonnie, then she wasn't as level-headed as he had thought.

Trego followed the road back across Ash

Creek Canyon, then cut across to the stage road. Reaching the canyon where he had been shot at yesterday, he reined down into it. His hand rested on his gun and his eyes moved quickly, determined to detect any movement. Today there was nothing. It was only after he had passed the spot where he'd been shot at yesterday that he began to relax.

Then he caught a movement under some trees off to his left. His gun whipped up as he realized a man was standing there. But the man was making no threatening moves toward him. He simply seemed to be staring in his general direction, hanging onto the tree as if he couldn't stand alone.

Trego rode closer, still wary of a trap. When he got close enough, he saw that the man really was clinging to the tree to keep from falling. He looked starved and as Trego swung down and got a level look at him, he saw that he was blind.

"What are you doing here, fellow?" he asked.

"I'm dying," the man said through thick lips. "I've got to have water."

Trego swung the canteen off his saddle and took it to the man, letting him have only a little at first. "How long has it been since you've had water?"

"I don't know," the man said in a smoother voice. "It's hard for me to tell time."

Trego realized that a blind man might have trouble telling day from night. "Are you hungry, too?"

The man nodded. "Where am I?"

"About three miles from Genesis," Trego said. "Who are you?"

"Zeb Myrick," he said. "I was coming to Genesis to rescue my twin brother."

"Web? Rescue him from what?"

"He's been kidnapped. I brought the ransom money, but somebody stole it from me."

Trego realized that he had fallen right into the answer to half his questions. Right now, he had to get Zeb Myrick to town and feed him and give him water. He likely needed a lot of rest, too. Trego would question him later.

"I'm going to put you on my horse," Trego said. "I live in town. I'm the preacher there. After I get you fed and rested up, I have a lot of questions to ask you."

"I've got some, too," Zeb said. "But I can't think well enough now to make sense."

Trego wished he could sneak Zeb Myrick into town without anyone seeing him, but that was unlikely. His mind was whirling with the possible answers to the questions that had been plaguing him.

In town, he took Zeb to the house and helped him inside, then told him to wait there until he got back. He went to the barn with his horse, then hurried back to the house. No one had been there. He gave Zeb more water and then some bread to eat while he got a fire going to cook some dinner.

After Zeb had eaten and had more water, he stretched out on the bed and Trego let him sleep, pushing back his curiosity. When Zeb stirred late in the afternoon, Trego got him up and let him have more water.

"Can you answer some questions now?" he asked.

"Sure, if you'll answer some for me."

"I'll do that if I can," Trego said. "First, I want to know how you heard that your brother had been kidnapped."

"I got a letter from somebody here in Genesis saying that he'd been kidnapped," Zeb said. "My sister read it to me. I was warned not to let anybody know about the letter or Web would die. It also said I had to bring a ransom of five thousand dollars to Genesis or he would die."

"Who were you to give it to?"

"The letter said I'd be told what to do

with the money when I got here."

The scheme was unfolding before Trego and he found it hard to believe. "You say you were robbed. Who did it?"

"I don't know anybody over here. I came on the stage; it's the only way I can travel. Something broke on the coach and we had to stop to fix it. Then some men rode up and pulled me off the coach and took me away. They took my money and were going to kill me but didn't because I'm blind."

"Did you hear them talk?"

Zeb nodded. "I'll recognize their voices if I ever hear them again. One wanted to kill me because that was their orders. The other one said there was no need to kill me. They'd just turn me loose down in the canyons and let me wander around till I died."

"They probably took you farther from town," Trego said.

"I figured that. I heard horses once, and I thought they might be going to town so I started walking in the same direction. I got so hungry and thirsty that I expected to die. Then I heard you."

"I'd guess you've been wandering for at least a couple of days out there," Trego said. "Now let me answer one of your questions even before you ask it. Your brother, Web, is all right out on his farm."

"But the letter said he had been kid-napped," Zeb insisted.

"That was so you'd bring the money. You're not the first one to be tricked like this. Somebody here knows the people back home who will dig up money to ransom these settlers. But the people who are sup-posed to be kidnapped aren't in any trouble at all. These thieves catch the fellow bring-ing the money, rob him and, I think, usually kill him.

"Nobody back home is the wiser because they don't know where the man has gone with the money. Nobody here suspects anything because nothing is wrong here. It's a clever scheme and might have kept right on working if they hadn't let you live. Of course, your sister might have told some-body when you didn't come back right away."

"She wouldn't have said anything for a long time," Zeb said. "She was afraid that Web would be killed if she did."

"They probably didn't know you were blind when they sent you that letter," Trego guessed.

He walked to the window and looked out at the deepening dusk in the street. The sun had gone down several minutes ago. He was almost certain now that his Uncle Luther had been robbed of his seven thousand dollars to ransom Pace Holcomb, and then killed. Even if Trego couldn't find Luther, he was going to find his killers and get that money back.

Wheeling around to Zeb, he said, "We'd better get you out to your brother's place tonight. If certain people find out you're here, you won't be safe."

"What people?" Zeb asked.

"If I knew that, we'd get a lot of things cleared up in a hurry," Trego said.

"How far is it out to my brother's?"

"No more than a couple of miles," Trego said. "We'd better go now."

He took Zeb by the hand and led him to the door. But as he stepped into the open doorway, a bullet splintered the doorjamb only inches from his head. He lunged backward, knocking Zeb down as he did.

"Who's shooting?" Zeb demanded from the floor where he had been thrown.

"Probably the same people who almost killed you out in the canyons," Trego said. "Keep down on the floor. They're not liable to hit you there. I'll see who it is."

Trego had just buckled on his gun belt, and now he lifted the gun from his holster and moved to the window. He was glad he hadn't lit the lamp. From the window, he stared out into the almost dark street. Apparently his return home today had been noted, but nothing had been done about it until dark. If Trego had put Zeb to bed here, likely he and Zeb would both have been burned alive shortly after dark.

The rifle roared again and the bullet thudded into the door that Trego had slammed shut. Another rifle from across the street shattered the window where Trego was watching. He ducked back. It was too dark out there to see anything more than the flashes of the rifles.

Then someone yelled over by the boardinghouse. "One of the Winchester Gang is holed up in the preacher's house. Help us smoke him out."

Trego watched for the next rifle shot and fired at the flash. Whoever had made that yell knew there was no Winchester Gang member in the house. If it was somebody who lived right here in town, his call might bring more people out to help capture or kill a member of that feared gang.

Trego was willing to bet some members of that gang did live right here in town. Somehow they were keeping the mail from going through. If just one letter from a relative like Ruth Holcomb got through to someone in Genesis, the people here would investigate and the plot would be uncovered.

That pointed the finger of suspicion to either the stage driver or the postmaster. Nobody else could sort a letter out of the mail. And it wouldn't be easy for the stage driver to get into that locked pouch. Trego didn't like to suspect Cal Oyler, but he remembered that letter Oyler had laid aside when he was cancelling mail that day to go out on the stage.

It made sense when Trego considered it. As long as nobody here heard about the worry back home, they wouldn't get suspicious. And people back home would never know that their relatives here were not in trouble so long as no letters got there to prove it. The only ones being hurt, Trego realized, were the messengers who brought the ransom money for relatives they thought had been kidnapped. They just never got to Genesis to find out about the hoax. Zeb Myrick was the exception. His appearance exposed the whole scheme, except to name the ones involved.

The shooting had practically stopped and Trego searched the street for some sign of the men who were holding him and Zeb Myrick prisoners. He saw a man ride into the street at the south end of town. It was too dark to recognize him, but as he moved up and men yelled at him to get out of the way, Trego thought he recognized the tall, stoop-shouldered farmer out south who had told him he'd seen Luther Holcomb just before he disappeared. He was probably in town to tell somebody that Trego had been inquiring about Luther. If Trego was guessing right on that, then the ring leader of this gang would soon know that Trego was more than just an innocent preacher. The gang would soon be as anxious to kill him as Zeb Myrick.

"Who's shooting at us?" Zeb asked, still hugging the floor.

"I can't see. But it's somebody who wants us dead. Just stay down. As soon as it's completely dark, we'll get out of here and I'll take you to your brother."

"I hope we can make it," Zeb said.

An occasional shot came from the area of the buildings across the street, just enough to let Trego know he couldn't risk leaving yet. He saw a big man dash across the alley between the deputy's office and the boardinghouse. There was no mistaking Grumpy Rush. Grumpy and Dett Skeen were sure to be two of the Winchester Gang.

Trego wished he could get up to Dibble's place. The druggist would help him. But if

Trego was to protect Zeb, he'd better get out of town with him. It was obvious to Trego now that his worst enemies were right here in town.

As darkness settled down, Trego kept a sharp vigil at the front window. The glass was gone from it now, knocked out by that rifle bullet early in the fighting. He could hear sounds in the street but those stopped, too, after dark.

Trego was aware of a whisper from Zeb and he turned his attention to the blind man. He was sitting up, his head cocked like an alerted dog. Trego moved noiselessly to him.

"Do you hear something?" he asked softly.

"Somebody is behind the house," Zeb said, turning his blind eyes that way. "Can't you hear him?"

Trego listened intently. He heard nothing. "Are you sure?"

Zeb nodded. "Something is moving out there. I hear him."

Trego recalled what he'd heard about blind people having exceptional hearing, compensating for their lack of sight.

"I'll check," he whispered and moved quietly to the back of the room.

He didn't expect anyone to be there, but the window was open and someone might be sneaking up to shoot them in the back or burn down the house. He was starting toward the window when he saw it darken as a bulk closed off the light. He still hadn't heard anything. Without Zeb's warning, he'd never have suspected a sneak attack from the rear. Trego shrank back against the wall and waited. The man didn't seem to have a gun but there was something in his hand. He made practically no noise as he climbed into the room.

Trego saw then that it was Furtak, and he had a club in his hand. He was intent on the sitting figure of Zeb in the middle of the floor.

# 10

Zeb Myrick had turned toward Furtak, apparently hearing him move. "Is that you, Sam?" he asked softly.

Furtak stopped at the sound of the name. Trego knew he had to act quickly. He didn't want to use a gun. He had a use for Furtak. Reaching down, he pulled a knife from his boot top where he'd been carrying it since he found that first threatening note here at the parsonage. Moving forward as quickly as he could, he pressed the point of his knife against the back of Furtak's neck.

"Drop the club," Trego snapped.

Furtak froze. Trego dug the point of the knife deeper. "Drop it!"

The club clattered to the floor. With his free hand, Trego searched Furtak for a gun. He wasn't wearing one, and Trego doubted if he had one hidden on him. Furtak was a man who killed with his hands or a club, not a gun.

Trego lifted his gun and jabbed it in the big man's back, returning the knife to its sheath.

"How many are out there?" he demanded.

"Enough to smoke you out of here," Furtak growled.

"You're going to be in the middle of that smoke now," Trego reminded him. "Where are they?"

"Go outside. You'll find out."

"If we go out, you'll lead the way," Trego said.

He pushed Furtak toward the window. Near the window Furtak hung back. There must be somebody watching for a shot through the window, Trego decided. Keeping the gun in Furtak's ribs, Trego searched the street. He saw movement at the deputy's office and at the corner of the boarding-house. That would pinpoint two of them. They were dim shadows, nothing to sight a gun on, but if he moved outside, they'd be ready for him.

"Do they figure on staying out there all night?" Trego asked.

"They'll burn you out long before morning," Furtak bragged.

"You'd better hope not, unless you want to roast, too."

"They know I'm in here."

128

"Then maybe they'll go easy with the matches," Trego said.

He had little hope of that. They'd expect Furtak to kill Zeb and Trego quickly, or else he'd give it up as too risky and report back to somebody out there who would then proceed to burn the house. Since Furtak wasn't reporting back, it should delay the fire for a little while. But soon they'd assume that Furtak was dead and go ahead with the burning.

"Zeb," Trego said. "We're going out. You take hold of my back pocket and follow me. If you lose me, drop flat on the ground and stay there till I come back for you."

"You're not really going to take me outside?" Furtak said, fear cracking his voice for the first time.

"You're going out the door first," Trego said. "If you're afraid of being shot in the front by your buddies, then I'll shoot you in the back."

Trego wasn't sure whether there would be anyone behind the house, but he intended to let Furtak find out. Maybe they'd recognize Furtak when he showed up in the doorway, but he doubted it. Trego was a little taller than Furtak and almost as broad. In the dark, it would be hard to tell the two apart.

Trego pushed Furtak toward the back door and ordered him to open it. He obeyed, and Trego decided that there likely wasn't any rifleman out there. Furtak didn't show the reluctance to go out the back door that he had when he thought they were going out the front.

With Zeb in tow, Trego pushed Furtak outside and along the back of the parsonage. The danger would come when they stepped into the alley between the parsonage and the church. Trego made sure that Furtak was the first one to move into the alley. He did it reluctantly, and hurried across to the rear of the church, Trego right with him, his gun pressing into his back.

At the church, Trego guided Furtak in the back door. If there was anybody watching the parsonage from here, he would surely be near the front.

"Can you handle a gun?" Trego asked Zeb.

Zeb said nothing, and Trego could barely see him nod.

"I've got this gun jabbed into Furtak's back," Trego told Zeb. "You keep it there. If he moves, blast him. Just remember, he was sneaking up to bash your skull in with a club."

"Don't leave me with him," Furtak pleaded.

"If you don't move, you'll be all right," Trego said.

He felt the firm hand of Zeb, and he didn't doubt that Furtak would be dead if he made a false move. Taking out his knife again, he moved down the aisle of the church to the front door. Carefully, he pushed the door open a crack. He almost caught his breath. There was a man not two feet away, peering around the corner toward the parsonage. Reaching through the half open door, Trego pressed the knife against the man's neck just as he had on Furtak.

"Back up," Trego hissed. He knew he'd attract some bullets if the men across the street saw too much movement here.

When the man hesitated, he dug the point of the knife in till the man squirmed and began backing. Trego opened the door enough that the man could step inside. There Trego took his gun and ordered him to lie down on the floor. He shut the door, then stepped over to a window where the women of the church had hung curtains and used small ropes to hold them back from the window when they wanted more light inside. Pulling one of the ropes free, he tied the man's hands behind him. He was a little man and when Trego rolled him over, he recognized Dett Skeen.

"If I'd known it was you, I might not have bothered to tie you," he said. "That knife would have cut some of the devilishness out of you."

Skeen glared at him through the dim light and Trego took the handkerchief out of Skeen's pocket and stuffed it in his mouth. Moving back to Zeb, he found Furtak standing as motionless as a statue.

"Looks like you've been a good boy," Trego said. He took the gun from Zeb and prodded Furtak. "Let's go."

"Where?" Furtak demanded.

"Ahead of my gun," Trego said. "Out the back door."

Furtak grumbled and moved slowly. As Trego passed the pulpit in the rear of the church, he thought that he'd had a gun in his hand here in the church almost as much as a Bible. It wasn't the way he would prefer it, but there was an element in this community that seemed to understand a gun much better than a Bible.

"Going back to the house?" Furtak demanded as they approached the back door.

Trego prodded Furtak harder. "You just worry about this gun," he said. "I'll worry about where we're going."

Once outside the church, Trego ordered Furtak to turn south toward the blacksmith shop. Furtak moved a little faster, apparently feeling he'd be on familiar ground if he got to his blacksmith shop.

At the corner of the church, Trego called a halt. There hadn't been much firing for quite a while. He knew they hadn't given up so they must be up to something.

Trego prodded the gun deeper into Furtak's ribs. "What are they planning to do?"

Furtak grunted and flinched away from the gun. "They're out to get you," he growled. "They'll do it, too, no matter how cute you think you are."

"Maybe they'll burn the blacksmith shop instead of the parsonage if we go there," Trego suggested. "Come on. Let's get over there."

There was a wide alley between the church and the blacksmith shop. Many people used it as a street. Trego thought that some of the men laying siege to the parsonage might use it as an avenue of approach to the rear of the house. He pushed Furtak out into the alley, not letting him get beyond the point of his gun. Nothing happened and he waited another minute to be sure, then, with Zeb holding to his hip pocket, he started across to the rear of the blacksmith shop. Nothing disturbed the silence of the alley as they reached the shop.

A yell sounded from the street then, coming from the boardinghouse corner, Trego guessed.

"Jumbo, where are you?"

Trego prodded the gun hard into Furtak's back. "You say one word and it will be your last," he said softly.

Furtak was quiet. Trego realized that Furtak's presence in the parsonage had stopped the guns. They had expected the big blacksmith to overpower those inside, and they wouldn't risk hitting him by firing at the parsonage while he was at his task.

Trego didn't see the horses standing behind the blacksmith shop until he almost bumped into them. He pushed Furtak up against the back of the building while he checked the horses. There were four, all saddled and standing around hitched.

"Whose horses?" Trego asked.

"They belong to the deputies," Furtak said. "You'd better not bother them."

"There's only one deputy here in Genesis," Trego said. "He may think he's important, but he's not big enough to need four horses."

"He deputized me and Grumpy and Dett to handle this trouble," Furtak said, a touch of importance in his voice.

Trego saw what Tom Ekhart meant when

he said Furtak was not too bright. Anyone who would take such pride in being deputized by Fred Petrauk and would brag about it under the present circumstances couldn't be too smart.

"What did you need horses for?" Trego asked.

"Me and Fred had to go out and round up Dett and Grumpy. We left our horses here when we got back."

Trego untied the rope from one of the saddles, an idea brewing in his mind. "Put your hands behind your back," he ordered.

While Trego tied Furtak's hands, the blacksmith made threats. As his voice got louder, Trego cut him off.

"Shut up or I'll cut your tongue out. That is a reasonable price to pay for your sins."

Furtak stopped his tirade, apparently believing Trego's threat. Leaving the blacksmith sitting against the wall of his shop, his feet bound, his hands tied behind his back, Trego went to the horses. He lifted Zeb into the saddle of one and mounted another. Tying the reins of the two remaining horses around the saddle horns, he gave each a hard slap on the rump and they charged out on the prairie beyond the blacksmith shop.

Clutching the reins of Zeb's horse, he

nudged the horse he was riding into a gallop. As they broke out from the protection of the blacksmith shop, Trego fired his revolver twice down the middle of the street. A few answering shots came out of the town but none came near him or Zeb. He saw men running in the street but he knew they wouldn't find their horses. It would take a while before they could get other horses and saddle them.

Cutting down into Ash Creek Canyon, Trego followed the road up the other side and on to Web Myrick's place. He dismounted, helped Zeb down, and left the puffing horses standing while he led the way to the door and knocked. Web Myrick answered.

After recovering from his initial surprise at seeing his twin brother, Web asked them to come in. Trego vetoed that.

"We're on the run," he said. "Right here is the first place they'll look for Zeb. We have to find a safer place for him."

"Tom Ekhart's," Web said without hesitation. "Uldine and I will come with you."

They rode back a short distance toward town, then turned south off the road to Ekhart's place. Only when they were inside Ekhart's house did Trego explain about finding Zeb wandering in the canyons, almost dying of hunger and thirst. He tried to get Zeb to tell his own story, but Zeb seemed confused as if the last few days had suddenly become a muddle to him. He didn't seem to remember the last few hours at all.

"It will come back to him pretty soon," Web said. "He used to forget everything if he got scared. Might be a day before he'd remember, but he always did. Besides, he's probably still mighty tired."

"And maybe hungry," Vona said.

She brought some bread and jam from the cupboard and Zeb did eat a little, but he did it almost as if he were in a trance.

"That was a terrible experience for him," Martha Ekhart said.

Trego repeated what Zeb had told him earlier, and the others agreed with his conclusion that this uncovered the extortion plot.

"It's almost certain that Uncle Luther is dead, robbed and killed by these murderers," Trego said. "If we only knew who they were!"

"Looks like Furtak is one," Ekhart said. "And Grumpy Rush and Skeen."

Trego nodded. "Petrauk just has to be one of them, too." He looked at Vona. "I think you should keep away from Furtak."

"Why?" she asked with a surprising show of independence. "I was only trying to learn some things from him."

"He may be stupid, but he's also dangerous," Trego said. "I don't think you're safe with him."

Vona started to make an angry retort and Trego realized she hadn't forgotten the story Yonnie had told about him and Alvena. Tom saved him by holding up a hand and silencing Vona.

"I agree with the preacher," he said. "Now that we know what Furtak really is, you shouldn't see him anymore."

"I wish we knew who else is involved," Web Myrick said. "None of the four we're talking about is smart enough to dream up a plan like they've working. Who could be the brains?"

"It's not Ivan Bridgewood," Tom Ekhart said. "And Cal Oyler is a good church going family man. The boy who runs the livery stable certainly isn't involved. That doesn't leave anybody we know except Horace Dibble, the druggist."

"Dibble has been a real friend to me," Trego put in. "I can't see him as a murderer. Whoever is running this scheme is a murderer whether he does the killing or orders it done."

Arrangements were made to keep Zeb at Ekhart's for a while with Web Myrick and his wife staying this first night until Zeb recovered his memory. Trego took his leave and rode to Pace Holcomb's to spend the night. He didn't trust the safety of the parsonage now.

Trego explained the situation to Pace and Katie and they faced up to the fact that Luther Holcomb was probably dead.

"Uncle Luther drew out seven thousand dollars before he left Sage Creek," Trego said. "Five thousand of that was mine, but two thousand was his own. I'm going to get that money back if I can find who took it. You and your mother can use the two thousand and I intend to buy a small ranch with mine."

"How are you going to find that money?" Pace asked.

"I think I can make Grumpy Rush talk if I can catch him away from his partner, Skeen. Tomorrow I'm going to ride over to his place and try to make him tell me what he knows."

"That will be dangerous," Pace said quickly. "You don't crawl into a wolf's den to catch a wolf."

"You do if you want him bad enough," Trego said.

# 11

Trego rode out of Pace's yard early the next morning, promising to let him know if he found out anything. He rode west past Ekhart's and Myrick's places without stopping. Crossing Spring Canyon, he took a left turn off the main road. According to Alvena's location of the homesteads over here, that one would be Grumpy Rush's place.

Trego approached the house cautiously. It was a half dugout with only one small shed close to the house. Grumpy apparently kept his horse there. Remembering how Grumpy had been shooting at his house last night, Trego kept his hand on his gun as he rode into the yard.

There was no stir. Before dismounting, he rode over by the little barn. There was a horse, but it was still saddled. That was one he had turned loose last night and run out of town. Grumpy must still be in town afoot.

Trego checked the house to make sure no

one was there. He took the saddle and bridle off the horse in the barn, then rode back to the main road. He stopped at Petrauk's place but no one was there, either. He thought of riding up to Skeen's, but he was sure now that place would be vacant, too. He really didn't want to see Skeen, anyway. He doubted if he could make the little gunman talk. And information was what he wanted now.

Instead of going back toward town, he rode on toward Guzek's ZK ranch headquarters. Yonnie might know something worth learning. He came in sight of the buildings, but before he reached them, he saw Oscar Coy down in a canyon cutting wood. He reined down the sharp incline to the spot where Coy was working. Coy watched his approach suspiciously.

"It's a long time till winter," Trego said, nodding at the ax and saw.

"Sure is," Coy said, wiping the sweat from his brow. "But Quint and Yonnie want plenty of firewood, and they believe in getting it in the summer instead of during a snowstorm."

Trego thought that Coy might be as good a source of information as Yonnie since he got his news from her. The stories that Yonnie told often ignored the truth, but in view of what he had learned from Zeb Myrick, maybe Yonnie's opinions of people in town would throw some light into new corners.

"What brings you out here, Preacher?" Coy asked, leaning his ax against a fallen tree trunk.

That was the moment when Trego saw the rattlesnake coiled against the rotting log. It was close to Coy. Another step and Coy would be within striking range of the snake. Trego jerked his gun out of his holster just as the snake issued its deadly warning. Coy leaped backward, almost falling. Trego didn't know whether Coy had jumped backward because of his move for his gun or because he heard the warning rattle of the snake.

Trego's shot buried itself in the coils of the rattler. The snake erupted into a frenzy of thrashing coils. Coy stood back aghast as the snake continued to writhe. Gingerly he reached out and got the ax. With half a dozen strokes, he had the snake cut into several segments.

Coy stepped back against the wagon he had brought to haul in the wood. He wiped a hand over his face. "That was close," he whispered. "I might not have seen him in time. Good shooting, Preacher."

"A lucky shot," Trego said. "I didn't have

time to aim." He swung down. The horse he was riding was the one he had borrowed in haste last night behind the blacksmith shop, and that shot had made him nervous.

"Lucky or not, I owe you for that," Coy said. "You sure are handy with that gun for a preacher."

"I haven't been a preacher all my life," Trego said. "I'm not so sure that I don't need this gun about as much as my Bible in order to be a preacher in Genesis, anyway."

"You're right about that. And if you need any help any time, just call on me. You've got a big favor coming."

Trego took the knife from the top of his boot and quickly cut off the rattles from the still writhing tail segment of the snake.

"You going to carry them things around?" Coy asked in horror.

"Maybe," Trego said. "I used to do that as a kid. Sure had a lot of fun with the girls. You could chase them with the rattles of a snake about as well as you could with a live frog or garter snake."

Coy shuddered. "I can't say that I blame them. When I hear those rattlers, even if they ain't hooked to a snake, I get the shivers."

"What do you know about the Winchester Gang?" Trego asked, dropping the rattles in his pocket.

"I ain't sure there is a Winchester Gang," Coy said. "We hear a lot about that gang. But I think it may be just a coverup for some sneaky crooked work in town."

Trego nodded. "Could be. Maybe those who keep talking about the Winchester Gang being in the country are the real gang. Is that possible?"

Coy rubbed his chin. "I reckon so. Never really thought of it that way, though."

"I'd like to know who you think might belong to that gang if it is made up of men in Genesis."

"That's a ticklish question. I could get my neck stretched for suggesting people if they found out about it."

"They'll never find out from me. I've already decided that the deputy, Fred Petrauk, and his two flunkies, Grumpy Rush and Dett Skeen, are three who qualify."

"I sure wouldn't quarrel with that. They're out and out thieves. They've stolen a chunk of ZK land, you know."

Trego nodded. "How about the blacksmith, Furtak? I've got him pegged as belonging to that gang, too."

"Could be," Coy admitted. "He's slow-witted enough to belong to anything that didn't require brains. He's also more scared

144

of a snake than I am. I saw him light out like his shirt tail was on fire one day when he saw a rattler."

"I'll remember that," Trego said. "Now I think you'll agree that none of those I mentioned are really smart enough to be the brains of a gang like the Winchester bunch. Who do you think would qualify as their leader?"

Coy shook his head. "You're backing me into a corner. Even if I had an idea, I sure wouldn't want to put it into names."

"I thought maybe Yonnie had said something."

"She says everything," Coy said quickly. "Some things that nobody in his right mind would repeat."

"Maybe I should talk to her. Isn't she suspicious of anybody in town?"

"Anybody?" Coy exploded. "She's suspicious of everybody. She says that Cal Oyler keeps secrets from his wife and daughter. She swears that Dibble cheats her when she buys anything at his store. She says that Furtak doesn't have as much sense as the horses he shoes. She says that Dibble is sweet on Alvena Oyler and Cal doesn't even know it. She thinks Vona Ekhart is a fool for letting that blacksmith get close to her. Now that's just a starter. I won't tell you what she says about you."

Trego didn't press the old man. He'd already told him some things that he needed to digest. Much of what he'd said, Trego already knew. But the fact that she thought Oyler was keeping secrets from his wife and daughter deserved some consideration.

"Have you ever thought of the stories you've heard about people starting to Genesis and not getting here?" Trego asked.

"Sure. That looks suspicious if it's true. You know anybody like that?"

"My uncle, Luther Holcomb, started here and didn't arrive. If you hear anything about him, I'd appreciate it if you'd let me know."

"You can count on that, Preacher. As I say, I owe you something."

Trego got on his horse and rode on. He had thought when he saw Coy that he'd just talk to him and go on. But now he decided that he might learn more if he did talk to Yonnie. Everyone told him that he couldn't believe anything she said. But she might be near enough to the truth that he could sift some accurate conclusions from her words.

Quint Guzek was just putting a team in the barn when Trego rode into the yard. He shut the door of the barn and came hurriedly over to where Trego had reined up.

"I want to tell you something, Preacher.

Yonnie got wind of that night you spent with Alvena Oyler. She loves that kind of gossip, you know. You could be out of a job by the time she gets that spread around."

"What did she hear?" Trego demanded.

"Somebody saw Alvena go to your place that night after you whipped Jumbo Furtak and nobody saw her come back."

"She did go back home just a short time after she got there," Trego said sharply. "You tell your wife she'd better get the facts before she spreads any story around."

Quint shrugged. "She never did bother much with facts. She likes a juicy story. I just thought if you knew, maybe you could dig up the proof of what really did happen and squelch her story."

Trego nodded, all desire to talk to Yonnie gone. "I'll think about that." He reined out of the yard and headed back toward town.

He was almost to town when he met Vona Ekhart driving a light spring wagon. She had apparently been to town for something. He slowed his horse, thinking she might want to talk a minute. But she turned her head away and slapped the lines over the horses' backs. He watched her, his lips in a grim line. Likely Yonnie had already spread her tale in town and Vona had heard it again.

Approaching town, he moved cautiously.

He was still riding the horse he had borrowed the night before. There had been some people in town last night who wanted him dead. They might organize a necktie party if they caught him riding this horse. He left the road as soon as he came up out of Ash Creek Canyon and angled for the corral behind the livery barn. There he tied the horse to the corner post and walked around to the front of the barn. He told Roger Sorenson about the horse outside, then checked to make sure his own horse was in the barn.

"That was Petrauk's horse you took," Sorenson said. "He was madder than a hen in a horse tank. The story's over town now that you found Web Myrick's twin brother and he'd been robbed. Is that right?"

Trego nodded. "That story, at least, is straight. We apparently have some first-rate crooks in town."

Trego hurried up the street. He watched for Petrauk. It would likely mean a showdown fight if the deputy saw him. But Trego didn't see a soul until he reached the drugstore. He opened the door and was met by the bulldog, King. Dibble was behind him and called the dog back.

"Things are a little sticky in town after that fuss last night," the druggist said. "I'm

148

glad you got away. Where did you take Web's brother?"

The caution that was always just behind Trego's thoughts kept him from telling all he knew. "I took him out to Web's place. But Web was sure whoever was trying to kill him would look there first so he decided to take him somewhere else."

Dibble nodded. "Smart move. I'm just glad he got away." His face lost its smile. "I also heard that Alvena spent the night with you after you whipped Furtak."

"Have you been listening to Yonnie, too?" Trego's voice was sharp. "Ask Alvena. She'll tell you she went back home right after she doctored my bruises."

Dibble nodded. "I believe you. No preacher would allow a girl to stay with him overnight in a small town like this."

"Or anywhere else," Trego added sharply.

Dibble held up his hand, his grin back on his face. "Sure, sure. But Yonnie spread the word all over town before she left yesterday. Better think of something to do or you'll be out of a job and Alvena won't have a friend left in town — except me. I believe what you said."

Trego thought of what Alvena had told him of Dibble's attentions to her. Yonnie had caught onto that gossip, too, according to what Oscar Coy had said. He doubted if Yonnie missed anything that was going on. Her trouble was that she reworked every story to make the juiciest piece of gossip possible before she retold it.

"I've got a sermon to get ready. I just felt like I wanted to talk to a friend first."

"You've got one right here anytime you need one," Dibble said. "By the way, I helped Roger Sorenson put a new pane in your window to replace the one that got shot out."

"I appreciate that," Trego said.

He went back down the street to the parsonage. Again he was extremely cautious as he went into the house. He was a marked man and the only way he was going to stay alive was to keep one jump ahead of his enemies. His biggest problem was that he couldn't identify all of them.

Until he left Guzek's ZK ranch, he'd had no idea what his sermon was going to be this Sunday. But now he knew. There were plenty of admonitions in the Bible against gossip.

He hadn't completely straightened up the house since he'd found it torn up the other day when he got home. Now he had trouble finding paper on which to make his sermon notes. In searching for paper, he finally looked behind the desk that had been there when he moved in. He saw a paper hanging from the back of the desk and he reached down for it. It was stuck to the back and tore when he pulled it free.

He looked at it carefully and discovered there was writing on it. Flour paste had been used to stick it to the back of the desk. It hadn't accidentally gotten stuck there as Trego had supposed. He spread the paper on the desk and smoothed the wrinkles out of it.

"Somebody is determined to kill me," he read. "I'm not sure who but if I find out, I'll put it —" There were some words missing where the paper had stuck to the back of the desk. Farther down beyond the tear he picked up the message "— so somebody can find the killer even if I am already dead."

Trego stared at the paper. He didn't recognize the handwriting, but he had no doubt that it had been written by Oliver Knowles, the minister who was here before Trego.

He pulled the desk out from the wall and carefully tried to scrape the paper off the back where it was stuck. But the words were on the inside and the paste held it tight. When it finally came free, there wasn't a piece of it big enough to patch together.

He'd give almost anything to know where Knowles was going to hide the information in case he found out who was after him.

Trego realized that he was probably in as much danger as Knowles had been. However, if he could find out what Knowles had learned, he might be able to identify his unknown enemies. That could save his life.

Tom Ekhart had guessed that Knowles had tried to identify the members of the Winchester Gang. From every indication, he had succeeded and had been killed because of it. Somewhere in this house might be the list of names, if Knowles had lived long enough after identifying them to make the list. At least, Trego knew now why his house had been ransacked. He hoped they hadn't found and destroyed that list.

Trego thought of the warnings he had received. He was certainly as near to death now as Knowles had been when he'd written this note.

# 12

Trego tried to concentrate on his sermon. Whenever he thought of Yonnie and her gossip, he found concentration easy. But then his mind would wander to the killers gripping this town. He wondered whose relative would be the next to die.

He was sure that this plan had been worked out carefully by a much smarter brain than that possessed by any of the men Trego had so far identified with the gang. The Holcombs had been victimized. Trego was sure that Luther was dead because of it. But Luther and Trego's savings were gone. The Greens had been victimized, too. Trego had held the funeral for Jim Green who had been robbed and killed while bringing money for the ransom of his uncle.

Zeb Myrick had been robbed, but not killed. That had been the gang's big mistake. It was logical that Zeb Myrick, blind and alone, would soon die out in those canyons.

But Trego's determination to find his uncle had taken him out there at just the right time to rescue Zeb. Now they all knew his story. What they didn't know was who was behind this plan of extortion and murder.

Trego thought of those he knew out on the homesteads. The only family he knew well that had not been hit by the scheme was the Ekharts. At least, nobody knew that they had been victimized. Apparently, when everything went exactly as the crooks planned, the people here at Genesis never knew that any crime had been committed. Pace Holcomb hadn't had an inkling that there was anything wrong until Trego told him that Luther was missing. Maybe the Ekharts had a relative somewhere who had received one of those ransom letters. Trego would have to check and see. There probably were other potential victims among people here in town and on the other homestead around. About the only people he knew so far were the ones who came to church.

There was one thing he could do that might or might not help. He could take Zeb Myrick back to the place where he'd found him and lead him around the area. He might feel or hear something that would be familiar or help him to remember something he had forgotten. It was worth a try. His memory was all right now, Web said.

But right now Trego had a sermon to get ready. He put everything else out of his mind and planned his sermon, making more elaborate notes than he'd used before.

Trego slept with a gun under his pillow and a knife on the bureau within reach of his hand. There was no interruption of his night's rest, although he had the feeling that eyes were watching his every move during the day.

Sunday morning came and he was at church before any of the congregation arrived. Again he was wearing his gun. He seldom moved out of his house without it anymore.

After Vona had led the congregation in three songs, it was Trego's time to step up to the pulpit. He chose his text from Judges, the fifteenth chapter and the fifteenth and sixteenth verses.

"And he found a new jawbone of an ass, and put forth his hand, and took it, and slew a thousand men therewith. And Samson said, with the jawbone of an ass, heaps upon heaps, with the jaw of an ass have I slain a thousand men."

Trego laid down the Bible and looked carefully over the crowd, letting his eye stop for a long moment on Yonnie Guzek sitting with her husband in the second row. His sermon was going to be short today but he thought it would be one the people would remember.

He quickly reviewed Samson's life and how much destruction he wrought against the Philistines when he turned loose his great strength. Then Trego remarked that people of today had that power; in fact, people sitting right before him had the power to kill their thousands. He pointed out that people's reputations were often as important as their physical lives.

"While Samson killed his thousands," Trego said sharply, "there are people today who are killing thousands of good reputations. They are being destroyed in the eyes of their fellow men by the jawbone of an ass."

A gasp swept over the congregation as they caught the meaning of Trego's words. Half the eyes in the church pivoted to center on Yonnie Guzek. Trego saw that she got the message, too. Wild fury was in her face, but she bit her lip and looked at her feet. If she spoke up now, she would leave no doubt that she understood she was being pointed out. That would be the equivalent of an admission of guilt.

Trego finished his sermon and asked if there were any announcements. Tom Ekhart stood up to announce that there would be a church picnic the following Sunday after services. In the afternoon there would be a discussion of the church's program, including a vote on the new preacher, whether to offer him a permanent job or not. Trego was sure of one "no" vote when he looked down at the Guzeks. He wasn't so sure about Quint Guzek. He was grinning like a cat with a pan full of cream.

After church, there were many sly references to his sermon and the point he had made. Quint and Yonnie Guzek left just as soon as Yonnie could get Quint out to their buggy.

Dibble shook hands with Trego at the door, a wide grin on his face. "You sure dehorned her," he said softly.

Trego got no reprimand from anybody on his sermon. He had expected it from some of the leaders of the congregation, such as Ivan Bridgewood or Tom Ekhart, but it was something he had been determined to say regardless of the consequences.

On Monday morning, he rode out to Ekhart's farm. Uldine Myrick had stayed with Zeb while the Ekharts were at church the day before. Now Trego wanted to take

Zeb out to the canyons to see if he could remember any more than he had already told him. Zeb was reluctant to go back, but he did want to help catch the culprits, so he agreed.

As Trego led Zeb's horse away from Ekhart's, he wondered how completely Zeb's memory had returned.

"Do you remember that night we were trapped in the parsonage and got away to come out here?" he asked.

"I remember being in the house with you when someone tried to sneak in the back way," Zeb said. "I don't remember much more till I was out here at Ekhart's."

"Do you remember what happened out in the canyons before I found you?"

Zeb nodded. "I remember everything up to the time I thought I was going to be killed there at your house. It's muddled beyond that. There seems to be something I want to tell you about that, but I can't quite recall what it is."

They reached the canyon where Trego had found Zeb. Trego explained where they were then they rode slowly down the canyon. Trego hoped they were backtracking the course Zeb had taken after being set afoot. A couple of miles down the canyon, Zeb held up his hand. The breeze was moaning softly through the trees of a side canyon.

"I remember this place," he said. "I remember the wind in those trees. This is where they left me after they decided not to kill me. They hit me over the head and rode away. I suppose they thought that lick on the head would confuse me until I couldn't follow them."

Suddenly Zeb stopped talking and listened. Trego listened, too, but he heard nothing.

"Somebody is coming," Zeb said softly. "Are we out of sight?"

"No," Trego said. "But we soon will be." He led Zeb's horse back into some cottonwood trees.

It was two minutes before Trego saw two riders coming down the canyon, moving easily, obviously unaware of the presence of anyone else. When they were close enough, he recognized Grumpy Rush and Dett Skeen.

"Be very quiet," Trego whispered to Zeb. "They're going to pass right close by."

This was a break Trego hadn't expected. Rush and Skeen were talking as they rode past. Trego had dismounted and held a hand over the nose of each horse. He just hoped that the horses passing didn't get wind of their brothers and whinny. They passed on without lifting their heads.

"Did you hear them?" Trego asked when the riders were gone.

"Like they were sitting across a table from me," Zeb said.

"Recognize the voices?"

Zeb shook his head. "These weren't the same voices I heard that day. The two men who brought me here were different in size; one spoke from up here, the other down there. So the one had to be tall, the other one shorter. It was the tall one who pushed me around, I think, because he was a big man."

"The two who just rode by fit that description. One is big as a skinned ox and the other is a little rat."

"I don't think they're the ones," Zeb repeated.

Trego was inclined to think that Zeb had just failed to recognize the voices. His first impulse was to go after the two and bring them back for Zeb to identify close at hand. It would mean a battle, but Trego was in no mood to shy away from that. The thing that did make him hesitate was the danger of leaving Zeb unguarded. What if Rush or Skeen evaded him and doubled back and got to Zeb? Or maybe someone else might come along. There were more people than

Rush and Skeen involved in the campaign to do away with Zeb.

His self debate was short and logic told him to stay and protect Zeb. The chance that Zeb was wrong in his voice identification was too slim to warrant the risk.

"Is there any other place in this canyon that you recall that we haven't been today?" he asked.

Zeb shook his head. "I don't remember much about places. I do recognize this place where they left me by the sound of the wind in the trees. There's nothing else I can recognize."

It had been a foolish idea, Trego decided, as they started back to Ekhart's farm. How could a blind man recognize things he couldn't see? Somehow Trego had hoped that locating a place he remembered would trigger other memories that would provide a clue as to who had robbed him and left him to die. If Trego believed what Zeb had said so far, then he was actually further from a solution than he had been. He had been guessing that Petrauk's two flunkies, Rush and Skeen, were the ones who actually committed the murders.

Just before they reached Ekhart's place, Trego saw the buggy in the yard. He didn't recognize it, but he couldn't take any chances. If the wrong people found out Zeb was staying at Ekhart's, it could mean trouble for the Ekharts and death for Zeb. Trego guided the horses around so the barn hid their approach. At the barn, Trego left Zeb, telling him where they were and why he wanted him to stay inside the barn.

Quickly Trego rode his horse around the barn and up to the house. Just as he dismounted, Jumbo Furtak backed out the door and Vona appeared in the doorway.

"I rented this rig from Rog Sorenson," Furtak said. "I don't intend to waste my money. We're going for a ride."

Vona shook her head. "I can't, Jumbo. I've got too much to do here."

Trego sized up the situation at a glance. Vona was following her father's instructions not to go anywhere with Furtak again. But Furtak was insisting and, recalling how he had performed at the dance, Trego didn't know what he might do if Vona continued to refuse to go.

"Come on!" Jumbo said sharply. "Let's go."

Trego crossed the yard in long strides. "You heard her, Furtak. She said she wasn't going."

Furtak wheeled like he'd been stung with a whiplash. "What are you doing here?"

"Seeing to it that Vona doesn't go anywhere with you," Trego said. "Are you going to argue the point?"

Furtak scowled at Trego, his slow mind groping for a solution. When it came, he backed away a couple of steps. Trego saw the balance swing in his favor and took advantage of it.

"You've got just one minute to get in that buggy and get out of sight," he snapped.

Furtak scowled harder and shuffled his feet. Then he wheeled and made for the buggy. Quickly he jerked the hitching rein loose and climbed in. Wheeling the team, he slapped the lines and left the yard in a whirl of dust.

Trego watched him go then turned back when Vona spoke.

"Thank you, Mr. Trego," she said softly. "Why did you do that? Was it because I go to your church?"

He shook his head. "I wasn't thinking of church right then. I don't like Furtak. And I do —" He stopped, realizing how he had backed himself into a corner. He did like Vona. He just didn't feel like this was quite the time to tell her so. He wasn't sure that his sermon Sunday had convinced Vona that Yonnie's gossip had been a lie.

Zeb came out of the barn, apparently feeling it was safe since he'd heard the buggy leave.

"That voice was one of them," Zeb said excitedly. "I know it was. That's what I wanted to tell you. I remember hearing it that night at your place."

"You mean Furtak?" Trego exclaimed. Trego's mind was racing. Zeb said that one man was tall. Furtak was tall. But then who was the shorter man?

"What does he mean?" Vona asked.

"He means that Furtak was one of the men who robbed him and left him in the canyons to die. He recognized his voice." Trego's mind leaped ahead. "I heard the women say they were going to clean the church tomorrow. Are you coming into town for that, Vona?"

"Of course. I always help with church work."

"I'll come out and ride in with you. I don't trust Furtak."

Vona didn't object. Trego took care of Zeb's horse, then rode into town.

He was back at Ekhart's the next morning at eight o'clock. Vona and her mother were ready and Tom had the spring wagon team hooked up. Trego rode beside the wagon into town. He didn't see Furtak but the blacksmith shop was closed as they came ito town. Trego felt that his time hadn't been wasted.

Other women came, including Alvena Oyler who gravitated to Trego as he tried to help with the heavy work. Trego saw Furtak come to his blacksmith shop, where he watched the church most of the morning, apparently not doing much work.

"Let's explore the cave next Sunday afternoon after the business meeting," Alvena suggested during a short break.

"What cave?" Trego asked.

"It's the one west of the bank," Alvena said. "There are all kinds of stories about it. Some say horse thieves used it as a hideout before Genesis started. Pa says the stage station agent before him found a crippled Indian hiding there after the army ran some Indians through here. It's a big cave."

Trego agreed that it would be exciting to explore the cave. Then when the cleaning was done, he rode home with Vona and her mother, and was glad that he did when he saw the way Furtak watched Vona as the spring wagon passed the blacksmith shop.

It was dark when Trego returned to town. He was in the depths of Ash Creek Canyon when he thought of the cave and looked up toward the canyon rim below the north end of town. He was startled to see a glow there as if there was a light back inside the bluff.

He reined up, considering investigating the light, but decided it would be wiser to wait till morning when he could see what he was doing. His first thought was that maybe prisoners were being kept in the cave. Since no one apparently ever went to the cave, that would be an ideal place to hide them. It was close to a food source at the store.

Trego went on home but his mind stayed on that cave. As soon as he had breakfast the next morning, he strapped on his gun and walked up to the bank then turned west to the canyon rim. He found a dim trail there that led down to the mouth of the cave. There was a fairly wide bench in front of the cave.

Trego stopped and examined the cave opening. There was no light showing inside now. Maybe it had been his imagination last night. Strange things happen when a man is on edge and it is dark.

He moved inside, wishing he'd thought to bring a lantern. This cave ran back far beyond the place where natural light could reach. He was back at the farthest reach of light when he heard a rock bounce just ahead of him. Had a foot knocked it loose?

# 13

Trego had his gun in his hand as he waited. But he heard nothing more. Moving silently forward, he stopped again to listen. There was still no sound. A rock must have dropped from the ceiling or wall.

If there were prisoners being held here, they must be farther ahead. He couldn't think of any other reason for a light being here the night before. Men had been in here. He had seen tracks out in front and fresh dirt along the walls of the cave before he got so deep into the cave that he could no longer see. He wondered why anyone would be digging in here.

He finally felt his way to a place where the floor sloped sharply upward. From the jumble of dirt and rocks, he decided he had hit the end of the cave. There was still no sign of any prisoners. Trego concluded that his idea of prisoners being held in the cave had just been wishful thinking. He'd hoped that by some chance Luther Holcomb might still be alive as a prisoner.

Carefully he picked his way back toward the mouth of the cave. He was still puzzled by the light he'd seen the night before, even beginning to doubt that he had really seen a light at all.

Reaching the mouth of the cave, he climbed back to the level of the town and went down the rim of the canyon to the corral behind the livery barn. Going inside the barn, he saddled his horse and rode out on the road toward Sage Creek. He no longer was looking for Luther; only Luther's grave.

Certain as he was that Luther was dead, he wanted tangible proof of the fact. Then he would concentrate on his search for the leader of this gang of murderers. When he found him, he'd find his money. Nothing short of death was going to stop him from finding his money and reclaiming it.

Turning off into the canyon where he'd been hung by the hands, he followed the trail where he'd taken Zeb a couple of days ago. He was sure that down here somewhere must be the place where the killers buried their victims.

He searched the floor of the canyon for any suspicious mounds of dirt and then moved back against the bluffs. He was in the mouth of the little side canyon where Zeb had remembered the whisper of the wind when a bullet spanged off a rock beside Trego's horse. The horse leaped forward and Trego let him go.

He headed for a grove of trees near a dry waterway in the middle of the valley. Another shot came his way, but it missed by a wide margin. Turning his head, he saw two riders in the little side canyon and recognized them almost instantly. Grumpy Rush and Dett Skeen. Why were they down here again?

They were riding hard after him, shooting as they rode. Neither was liable to hit much from the back of a galloping horse. Anger surged through Trego. He'd suffered enough misery because of those two. He had a rifle in his saddle boot and he jerked it out, then wheeled his horse directly toward the two. Pumping a cartridge into the chamber, he kicked his horse into a gallop straight at Rush and Skeen. He fired twice before they broke their charge. They evidently thought they had Trego on the run and they'd follow until they got in a lucky shot. They didn't relish the situation when the tables were turned.

By the time the two got their horses turned around, Trego was within close rifle range. The two spurred their horses into a dead run. Skeen, with a faster horse, pulled away from Rush. Trego gained on Rush. Those two were down here for some reason. He intended to find out what it was.

Grumpy was ten yards behind Skeen when his horse stumbled and fell. He was thrown over his horse's head. The horse got up, unhurt, and trotted a few feet away. Skeen turned to look, but he didn't slow his horse.

Trego stopped his horse when he reached the man on the ground. When Grumpy rolled over, clawing for his gun, he found himself staring into the muzzle of Trego's rifle.

"I've got some questions to ask you," Trego said. "Drop the gun and get up. If you want to live, you'll tell me about the men who have been buried out here in these canyons."

"I don't know nothing," Grumpy whimpered, getting to his feet and leaving his gun on the ground.

"Who's been killing the people coming to Genesis?"

Grumpy shot a glance at Skeen just disappearing up the canyon. "Who's been killed?" he mumbled.

"I know about the whole scheme," Trego

said impatiently. "Now unless you want to die out here, too, you'd better start talking. Where are the graves of those who were killed?"

Trego could tell by the expression on Grumpy's face that he had hit on something he knew. After hearing from Zeb that Furtak was the big man who had almost killed him, Trego had ruled out Grumpy as one of the killers. He was sure now that he wasn't. His face was like an open book. When he didn't know an answer, it was plain to see in his blank face. He didn't know who did the killing. But he did know where the graves were.

Trego motioned with the muzzle of his rifle. "Catch your horse. You're going to show me those graves."

Grumpy scowled, but he didn't refuse. Perhaps he could read as much in Trego's face as Trego could in his. He walked over and got the reins of his horse and mounted.

"I'll keep this rifle on your back. One wrong move and there'll be another grave."

Grumpy rode carefully, making no unnecessary moves. He continued up the side canyon in the direction he had been going. In a low spot where sand and dirt had collected from rain water rushing down the canyon, Grumpy pulled up. There were four low mounds in a row. They were hidden behind some chalk rocks that had fallen off the canyon rim. Anyone casually riding by wouldn't be likely to notice them.

"Whose graves are they?" Trego demanded.

"I don't know," Grumpy whimpered. "This place scares me."

"Who is in that newest one?" Trego asked, pointing. "If you don't know, you're going to have to dig down and see."

"I can't do that," Grumpy whispered. "He's — he's dead."

"Dig!" Trego snapped.

Grumpy looked over at Trego and the gun he was holding. Trembling, he climbed off his horse and went to the mound. Before he started digging, he looked back at Trego again. Then he started clawing at the dirt.

It was a very shallow grave. As soon as Grumpy had uncovered one arm and Trego saw the sky blue sweater that he remembered so well, he knew that he had found Luther Holcomb's grave.

"Cover it up," Trego ordered. "Then pile some rocks over it. A coyote could dig that out. Do you know who killed these men?"

"No," Grumpy said as he hastily threw dirt back over the grave.

Trego had no reason to doubt his vigorous denial. "Who do you take your orders from?"

"I work for the deputy sheriff, Fred Petrauk."

"Did Petrauk kill these men?"

Grumpy carried some chalk rocks from the bluff and laid them on the grave he had finished refilling. "I don't think so. He didn't seem to know about these graves when Dett and I stumbled onto them and told him."

Satisfied that he had learned all he could from Rush, Trego told him to get back on his horse. "I'll take you down to Sage City tomorrow to the sheriff. You tell him what you told me."

Sullenly, Grumpy started back down the canyon, but Trego saw the fear in his face. They were just climbing up out of the canyon to the main road when three riders appeared in the canyon below. They had rifles and they opened up on Trego. Trego recognized Skeen, but he didn't have time to identify the others. They knew how to use rifles, that was certain. At first sight of the riders, Grumpy had broken back toward them, leaning far over his horse. Trego let him go. He'd be lucky to get out of this canyon alive without worrying about holding his prisoner. He kicked his horse into as fast a run as he could manage up the slope to the road. Once Grumpy was back with the group, they seemed more interested in him than in chasing Trego.

Trego was slowly unraveling the mystery, but he still didn't know the man he had to find if he was going to get his money back. He thought of that list the preacher Knowles had said he would make. Had he actually made the list? Where had he hidden it?

Trego spent the rest of the afternoon and evening looking through the parsonage and came up empty-handed. He rode out the next morning to tell Pace about finding Luther's grave, then returned to his search. By late afternoon, he'd about decided that Knowles hadn't lived to make his list. Then a sharp rap on the door broke his concentration. Oscar Coy stood outside, practically jumping up and down in his impatience.

"Come quick!" he said the second Trego opened the door. "We've got to save Quint!"

"Quint Guzek?" Trego said. "What's the matter?"

"We caught Grumpy and Dett branding ZK calves this morning," Coy said hurriedly. "There was some shooting and Quint killed Dett Skeen. Now Quint's at the deputy's office demanding that Petrauk arrest Grumpy. You know that Skeen and Petrauk were as thick as thieves. Petrauk wants the whole ZK. He'll kill Quint if we don't stop him."

"I'm a preacher, not a lawman," Trego objected.

"Come on," Coy screamed. "I know you can use a gun. I saw you."

Trego grabbed his gun and followed Coy. For an old man, Coy could move remarkably fast. They reached the front door of the deputy's office just in time to hear Guzek yell that he'd have the sheriff at Sage Creek take away Petrauk's deputy star.

Both men were so intent on their argument that they didn't notice the arrival of Trego and Coy. Guzek was wearing a gun, but he seemed unaware that he even had it. Petrauk was livid with rage and he had his hand on his gun.

"Nobody threatens the law and gets away with it!" Petrauk shouted.

The deputy jerked his gun free of the holster. Trego shouted at him from the door.

"Drop it, Petrauk!"

Surprise halted the deputy's move. He wheeled to face Trego's gun. He saw something in Trego's face that caused him to let his gun drop to the floor.

"I'll see you hang for this, Preacher!" Petrauk snapped. "Nobody can come into this town and threaten the law."

"Looks like we just did," Trego said. "Come on, Mr. Guzek. Get out of here."

Quint Guzek moved toward the door, his rage of a minute ago gone as he saw the gun the deputy had dropped. He stared from it to Trego and back to Petrauk.

"He was going to kill me," Guzek said in disbelief.

"I told you," Coy said. "Come on." He stepped in and picked up Petrauk's gun. "I don't want you shooting us in the back as we leave."

"You'll all hang for this!" Petrauk shouted.

They hurried across the street. Trego kept his gun in his hand and watched for Petrauk. The deputy surely had other guns in his office. He was furious enough now to shoot any one of them he could get in his sights.

They had just gotten into the parsonage when the back door opened and Ivan Bridgewood popped in.

"I saw what happened," he said. "You'd better bed down at my place tonight, Preacher. I don't trust Petrauk as far as I can see a dime on a dark night."

Trego nodded. "Might be a good idea. What about Mr. Guzek?"

"We've got our horses on the other side of the boardinghouse," Coy said. "We'll go out the back and around the church and blacksmith shop before we cross the street. We'll get home all right."

As they left, Trego turned to Bridgewood. "I'll be over as soon as it's dark. I want Petrauk to think I'm staying here."

Bridgewood nodded. "Smart idea."

From his window, Trego saw Coy and Guzek disappearing on the road down into the canyon. A short time later, he saw Petrauk leave his office and go down to the livery barn, then cut across to the blacksmith shop. Trego got some supper. Then, with shadows covering his movements, he went out the back door and over to the banker's house.

Bridgewood had an office in his house that had no outside windows. Trego was directed to that. He'd sleep there tonight. The banker wanted to know what he had learned.

"I found my uncle yesterday," Trego said. "Buried out in the canyons. Uncle Luther had seven thousand dollars, five thousand of it mine, that he was bringing to ransom Pace. I'm going to get that back. I just have to find the leader of this gang of murderers."

"Petrauk?" Bridgewood suggested.

Trego shook his head. "I don't think he's smart enough. Neither is Furtak. Since no letters get through, it seems that either Cal Oyler or the stage driver, Adalbert, might be involved."

"Cal's a good bank customer," Bridgewood said. "Seems honest enough."

Mrs. Bridgewood came to the study. "Somebody is sneaking around the parsonage," she announced.

"Douse the light like we're going to bed," Bridgewood said. "We'll take a look."

With the light out, they went to the window. Trego saw two men sneaking up to the rear of the parsonage. Suddenly, it struck him that these were the men who wanted to get rid of him because he already knew too much. If he could capture one and make him talk, he might get the name of the leader.

"I'm going out there," Trego announced.

"Don't be a fool," Bridgewood said. "You're out of their trap now."

"Those men know who the leader of this outfit is. I've got to know."

Bridgewood evidently saw the determination in Trego because he nodded. "Go out this back door. You can come back in the same way."

Checking his gun, Trego slipped outside.

From the corner of the house, he studied the scene. There were only two men near the back of the parsonage. One was a big man. That would be either Grumpy Rush or Furtak. He didn't want either one of those. Rush didn't know anything and Furtak probably wouldn't talk if he did know. The other man was closer to Trego, anyway. He was a tall slim man. He must know what was going on or he wouldn't be here, Trego reasoned.

Leaving the corner of the house, he moved forward with all the stealth he could muster. The big man off to Trego's left was almost around the corner of the parsonage now. The man he was closing in on was close to the near corner.

He was within three feet of the man when the man wheeled suddenly and Trego pointed the gun directly into his face.

"Don't make a sound!" he hissed. He recognized the stage driver, Buck Adalbert. He was a friend of Cal Oyler's. If Oyler was involved, Adalbert would know. Adalbert, however, had no intention of surrendering. He yelled. Trego brought his gun around in an arc, clipping Adalbert on the side of the head.

But the damage had been done. He heard yells from the front of the parsonage and from the far corner. He'd be caught in a crossfire.

# 14

Trego didn't wait for them to get a line on his position. He'd be a fool to take on the whole bunch. There must be three or four more besides Adalbert.

Keeping as low to the ground as possible, he scooted back toward Bridgewood's big house. He was almost to the corner when one of the men out in front saw him and fired a shot his way. It missed, but Trego knew there wouldn't be too many misses at that range. He heard the men running behind him as he went around the corner. He didn't want to bring trouble to the banker but Bridgewood's house was his only hope of escaping. He ducked through the back door of the house and pulled the door shut behind him.

"Get in my study and don't make a sound, no matter what happens," Bridgewood said.

Trego dodged into the inner room and dropped on the floor facing the door. If they came into the banker's house and opened that door, they'd be in for a real surprise.

He heard somebody knock on the back door and Bridgewood answer. After a short argument, the man outside admitted he hadn't seen Trego come into Bridgewood's house but there wasn't any other place where he could have disappeared so quickly.

Bridgewood professed ignorance of Trego's whereabouts and suggested that he might have made it to the drugstore. When the men were gone, Trego slipped out of the room.

"Think they'll come back?"

"Maybe," the banker said. "But they'd better not break into my house."

"If I was gone, you could let them in to look. Then they wouldn't bother you anymore."

"Just where would you go? And how?"

"Do you know where they are now?"

"Two of them are out front near the parsonage corner. One is just coming back from the drugstore. He's close to my back door now."

"I'll go out a north window," Trego said. "They might burn your house if you don't let them search the place."

"I'll kill some of them if they try," Bridgewood said.

"That won't save your house." Trego went to a bedroom on the north and looked outside. There didn't seem to be anybody on this side. Since there was no door here, they might not watch this side.

Quietly, he lifted the window. Bridgewood came in with a revolver in his hand. "If anybody shows up, I'll plug him," he whispered.

Trego let himself down outside the window. He could see a light in Dibble's house behind the drugstore. He might find refuge there, but he didn't want to jeopardize any more of his friends tonight. He heard a heavy knocking on the front door of the banker's house. This time Bridgewood could let the men inside to search. That should save him a lot of trouble.

He slipped over to the drugstore and went behind it. On the other side, he crossed the street, ducking in behind the town hall. He hadn't seen anybody over in front of Bridgewood's. He supposed they were inside looking for him.

Quickly he made his way behind the town hall, the deputy's office, and the boardinghouse. At the livery barn, he climbed into the corral then went in the back door. He was surprised to find Roger Sorenson there.

"Looking for a place to hide?" the livery

man asked.

"I'd rather fight than hide," Trego admitted. "But I don't like the odds. I want to find out just who is the brains behind these flunkies."

Sorenson nodded. "Since Zeb Myrick showed up, we're all wondering what is going on. Climb up into the loft. I'll make sure nobody finds you."

Trego climbed the ladder to the loft and snuggled down in the hay where he could keep an eye on the top of the ladder leading up to the loft. Trego had almost dropped off to sleep when he heard a loud voice at the front of the barn. It was Petrauk.

"Is that so-called preacher here?"

"Why would he be here?" Sorenson countered. "This is no church."

"He tried to kill me today. Nobody does that to the law in this town. I'm going to search this place. The coward is hiding somewhere."

"Look good," Sorenson called loudly. "Maybe you'll find that old fork I lost."

Trego, eyes accustomed to the dark, saw Petrauk hesitate at the obvious warning, then come on into the barn and move cautiously down the alley between the stalls. He stopped at the foot of the ladder and looked up. Trego waited, his gun in his hand. But Petrauk turned and headed back toward the door. Trego guessed he was afraid he might find him up there in the loft. Trego settled down, feeling that he probably wouldn't be disturbed now that Petrauk had looked inside the barn.

He came down from the loft as soon as dawn filtered into the barn. He'd had a fairly good night, considering the fact that he'd never completely relaxed. Slipping across the street, he went back to the parsonage. It was undisturbed. He was sure it wouldn't have been if they hadn't seen him last night after he knocked out Adalbert and known he wasn't in the house.

He had just stepped out of the house after breakfast when he saw Petrauk coming across the street toward him. He waited, watching the deputy's gun hand. But Petrauk didn't appear primed to test Trego's skill with a gun.

"This is the day you leave Genesis," Petrauk said when he was within twenty feet of Trego. "By Sunday you'll either be gone or dead."

Petrauk turned and started back toward his office without waiting for Trego's reaction.

"If you want me gone," Trego called after him, "why don't you arrest me now and take me down to Sage Creek?"

"I've got better things to do now," Petrauk said, not stopping. "But you'd better be gone by the time I finish."

Trego wondered if he was up to something else or if Petrauk was just afraid to force the issue. Trego turned up the street. He didn't have much time to locate the leader of this gang of murderers. He'd talk to Dibble again. Maybe he could tell him something that would give him a clue. If he didn't find the outlaw leader, he had no chance of getting his five thousand dollars back. And he had no intention of leaving here without it.

Horace Dibble had just opened up his drugstore for the day. Trego headed for the door and was met there by the big white bulldog. No matter how often Trego encountered that bulldog, it seemed that he got no friendlier. He looked and acted like he hated everybody.

"It's all right, King," Dibble said from the back of the store. "Come on in, Preacher. What can I sell you this morning?"

Trego stepped past the bulldog into the store. "I'm looking for advice again."

"I've got lots of that. It's cheap."

"I had a run-in with Petrauk yesterday, trying to save Quint Guzek's life," Trego said. "A bunch of roughnecks tried to kill me last night. I managed to give them the slip. I'm sure Petrauk was one of them. Do you think it's possible that the deputy is the ring leader of the Winchester Gang?"

Dibble came out from behind the counter where he'd been dusting off some items on the shelf. "I'm not even sure that there is such a thing as the Winchester Gang. I've heard talk about the gang but I've seen no evidence of it."

"What about those graves out in the canyons?" Trego asked.

Dibble's jaw dropped. "Graves? What graves?"

"Grumpy Rush showed me four graves. One of the men buried there is Pace Holcomb's father. Those men didn't kill and bury themselves. They were surely the victims of the Winchester Gang. Maybe they don't call themselves that. But somebody robbed and murdered those men."

"I'd never heard of that," Dibble said. "How come Pace Holcomb didn't mention it?"

"He didn't know about it," Trego said. "But the graves are proof that somebody around here is a murderer. It looks like a gang to me. If so, who in this town would be involved?"

Dibble frowned. "Maybe Jumbo Furtak,"

he said finally.

Trego nodded. "That's one. I'm also sure that Petrauk and his two shadows, Rush and Skeen, are in for it. Skeen's dead now. Do you think Petrauk could be the leader?"

"I doubt it," Dibble said. "He's not too brilliant, as you know."

"What about Adalbert, the stage driver? He was one of those trying to get me last night."

"Hard to believe he's involved," Dibble said. "He's in town only half the time so he's not likely to be the leader."

Trego nodded. That made sense. But it left him with no new clues. "How about Cal Oyler?" Trego asked, watching Dibble's reaction.

The druggist shook his head. "I can't believe that. He's in church every Sunday, you know, just like me."

Trego nodded. "I don't like to think it of him. But somebody is the brains. The scheme he dreamed up is not the work of a fool."

"If you're facing an unknown enemy here in town, you might do well to get out while you're still alive."

"I can't do that," Trego said, shaking his head. "Somebody here has five thousand dollars of my money and I intend to get it back. Petrauk threatened me just a few minutes ago. Said I'd either be gone or dead by Sunday morning."

"Well, if you're determined to stay, you know you can depend on me for help," Dibble said.

"How much stock would you take in Petrauk's threat?"

Dibble shrugged. "Not too much. He's mostly blow. But I'd watch him. He can't be trusted."

"I'll do that," Trego said and headed for the door, stepping around the big bulldog.

Trego watched for Petrauk during the day, but didn't see any sign of him. Maybe he had gone on that errand he had hinted he had to do. Or maybe Dibble was right. Maybe Petrauk was all blow and was avoiding a face to face encounter with Trego. Trego wouldn't let down his guard, anyway. A man like Petrauk would take advantage of any chance to shoot an enemy in the back.

As the day wore on, Trego tried to concentrate on his self-assigned task for the day, getting his sermon ready for Sunday. This was Friday. If he wanted to stay on in Genesis as a preacher, he'd better have a good sermon ready for Sunday's service. The vote was that afternoon. He could feel sure of one vote against him. Yonnie Guzek would hardly vote for him after his sermon on gossip last Sunday.

He was thinking of Yonnie when he heard a team running up the street and stepped to the window. Yonnie Guzek was standing in the front of a wagon, slapping the lines on her team as the horses dashed past the livery barn on their way into town. Yonnie began to haul the team down as they passed the church. She got them stopped in front of Bridgewood's house. Trego ran out the door. He couldn't see what was in the wagon, but something was wrong to cause Yonnie to drive like that.

He was the first to reach the wagon. "What happened, Mrs. Guzek?" he asked.

She glared at him a second then burst out, "Quint's been shot. And there ain't any doctor here."

Trego stepped up on a wheel and looked into the wagon. Quint Guzek was stretched out in the wagon bed, a blanket under him and another over him.

"Take him into my house," Trego said. "Then find the deputy. He'd know where you can find a doctor."

"That stinking deputy is the one who shot him!" Yonnie screamed. "Him and that no-good Grumpy Rush!"

Trego went around to the back of the

wagon. The endgate was gone. Likely Yonnie hadn't taken time to put it in. It was reasonable that Petrauk was the one who had shot Guzek. They'd had that run-in yesterday. Petrauk wouldn't let that go unanswered. And it was no secret that Petrauk wanted more of the ZK ranch than just the homestead plot he had taken. With Guzek dead, he might think he could just move in and take over.

Dibble came running from the drugstore just north of Bridgewood's house. He helped Trego carry Quint Guzek into the parsonage.

"Don't take him in there!" Yonnie screamed.

Trego ignored Yonnie and led the way to the bed in the big guest room where they laid the rancher.

"Where's Coy?" he asked.

Yonnie scowled at Trego from the doorway. "He went to Sage Creek for the doctor. But he can't get the doctor back here before tomorrow sometime."

Trego looked over the old rancher. The wound was high in the chest and apparently the shot had come from close range. The bullet had torn its way out his back. Trego was no authority on wounds, but this one looked clean. It all depended on what it had hit on its way through the chest. If it had hit nothing vital, the chances of recovery were good.

Alvena Oyler came to the door. She had seen the commotion and wanted to know if she could help. Trego put her to work bathing and bandaging Guzek's wound.

"Is that weasel who calls himself a deputy sheriff in town yet?" Yonnie asked after a while, staring across the street at the deputy's office.

"I haven't seen him since this morning," Trego said.

"He wants the whole ZK ranch," Yonnie said. "It's galling enough to have him and them other two parasites take those homesteads on the best grass on the ranch, but then they steal our cattle to get their herd started. Now Petrauk thinks he can take over the whole ranch." She fingered the rifle she had grabbed from the wagon when she came in. "He won't get it. I'll kill him myself. I'm going to go look for him right now."

"I think you ought to stay here," Trego said. "Your husband may come to and call for you."

Trego didn't really expect her to stay, but she turned to look at Quint then stood the rifle in the corner and went to sit beside him. There was genuine concern on her face.

Ten minutes later, Cal Oyler came hurrying down the street and stopped at the parsonage. Seeing Alvena inside, he stepped in. "Come on home, Alvena. This is no place for you. It's not safe."

"Why not?" Trego asked quickly.

"Dibble says that Yonnie thinks Petrauk shot Quint," Oyler said.

"That's what she says," Trego agreed. "Do you think Petrauk would shoot Alvena if he found her here?"

"I don't even think Petrauk shot Guzek," Oyler said. "He's a good deputy."

"He's a good killer!" Yonnie exploded from her seat at Quint's bedside.

Oyler ignored her. "Come on, Alvena."

Alvena went reluctantly. They had barely turned up the street when Trego saw Roger Sorenson hurrying up from the livery barn. He went outside to meet him.

"The deputy and Grumpy Rush just rode in on tired horses," Sorenson said. "Petrauk said that Yonnie Guzek is after him."

"For a good reason," Trego said. "He shot Quint."

"I saw her drive in. I figured something was wrong."

"Better tell Petrauk not to show up at the

193

front of his office if he wants to stay alive," Trego said. "Yonnie has a rifle over here."

Trego watched Sorenson hurry back. He really wouldn't cry if Yonnie did shoot Petrauk, but he couldn't deliberately let it happen.

The afternoon faded into evening. The Bridgewoods came over. Mrs. Bridgewood sat with Yonnie while Quint recovered consciousness but didn't stir much. Ivan Bridgewood offered to help Trego stand guard during the night. Both men knew that the danger wasn't past as long as Petrauk had a chance to get to Quint Guzek.

It was during Trego's turn at watch that he smelled coal oil and rushed to the door. That smell could only mean one thing. Someone was trying to set fire to the house.

# 15

Carrying his gun, Trego stepped outside and ran to the side of the house. The odor of coal oil was stronger here. He saw a man running around the corner of the church. He was gone before Trego could even yell at him.

He located the can that the man had dropped and found the place on the bottom boards of the house that had been splashed with coal oil. Running back into the house, he brought out the water bucket and sloshed it over the spot. If he left that coal oil there, whoever had put it there could sneak back any time in the night and touch a match to it. The water washed off the coal oil and soaked the boards so they wouldn't be likely to burn.

When he got back inside, Bridgewood was awake, too. They discussed this new threat and decided they would both stand guard the rest of the night, one near the front of the house and the other near the back.

The remainder of the night passed without incident and Yonnie got breakfast for all of them, inviting Mrs. Bridgewood to stay when she came over to find out when her husband was coming home. Quint Guzek was neither better nor worse. Mrs. Bridgewood said that was a good sign. He was going to make it whether the doctor got there or not.

Trego went to the front door and looked out. He studied the deputy's office directly across the street for some time. There seemed to be no movement there. He wouldn't have been surprised to find Petrauk stationed there ready to shoot anybody who came out. He wanted to get rid of Quint Guzek, but he was equally eager to kill Trego.

Satisfied that there was nothing stirring at the deputy's office, he switched his attention to the boardinghouse. He saw no open windows facing him and there was nothing within sight at any corner of the building. He opened the door and stepped out on the porch. His eyes swept the street.

Some movement caught his eye as he looked toward the church. He stepped quickly back inside the house without waiting to identify or even locate that movement. He had barely caught it and it seemed to be above him. Going to a south window, he studied the church. There were two windows on the north side of the church, but neither would have been in his view from the front door. His eyes moved up to the roof of the church and then on to the empty bell tower. That must have been where he thought he'd seen movement.

He studied the belfry carefully. The crossbar from which the bell would hang, if they ever got one, was visible. The platform below it had a waist-high wall around it. The upper part where the bell would hang was open so the sound of the ringing bell would carry over the town.

As he watched, he saw a man's head poke up above that low wall just for an instant. That was what he had seen. He'd been lucky that he hadn't stepped to the outer edge of the porch. He'd have been in full view of that belfry then. He didn't need anyone to tell him that the minute he stepped away from the house this morning, he was ticketed for death.

He gave the situation some careful thought. There was no way he could get out the front door and escape that marksman. If he went out the back door, he might dodge across to the back of Bridgewood's house and on to the drugstore. But the belfry was tall. The man up there had a clear view of most of the town. The minute Trego moved away from a building, he'd be within sight of that rifleman up there.

He couldn't stay cooped up here all day. He went to the back of the house. Bridgewood asked what was wrong and Trego explained. Yonnie and the banker and his wife went to the window and looked up. Trego suggested that they not let the man up there see them. He'd know then he'd been discovered and he'd be even more alert. Trego had a plan to surprise him.

Going out the back door, Trego hugged the house. The parsonage was between him and the belfry now. His dangerous moment would be when he dodged across to the church. From the corner of the house, he peeked cautiously up at the belfry. When he saw the man raise his head for a look, he ducked back. But he'd seen something he hadn't noticed before. The man had white hair. That was Jumbo Furtak in the belfry.

When Furtak dropped down again, Trego scurried across the gap between the parsonage and the back of the church. He drew no fire, and he was certain he had made the crossing without detection. Sneaking in the back door of the church, he made his way quietly toward the front to the foot of the ladder leading up into the belfry. Looking up, he could see no sign of Furtak.

Just before he started to climb the ladder, he remembered what Oscar Coy had said about Furtak being deathly afraid of a rattlesnake. Trego still carried those rattlers he'd cut off that snake he'd killed. He took them out of his pocket and held them in his hand.

He couldn't carry a gun in his hand very easily as he climbed and when he got to the top, he'd have to do something to divert Furtak's attention for just an instant if he wanted a fair chance at the big blacksmith. These rattles might create that diversion.

He climbed the ladder slowly, careful not to make any sound. When he was within two steps of the top, he paused and lifted his gun. With his left hand he tossed the snake rattles up through the hole in the floor at the top of the ladder. The rattles hit the floor of the belfry and rattled all the way to the far wall. Trego leaped up the next two steps and poked his head and gun through the hole of the belfry platform.

He didn't use his gun. Things were erupting before his eyes. Furtak apparently had been standing up in the belfry, leaning out to see something toward the rear of the parsonage. Maybe Bridgewood had created some kind of diversion there, guessing what Trego was trying to do.

When the rattles struck the floor, sounding very much like an angry rattlesnake, Furtak had apparently panicked. He had lunged away from the sound just as Trego got his eyes above the level of the floor.

In lunging backward, Furtak had thrown himself half over the low wall around the belfry. Now he was struggling to pull himself back. But he had gone too far. Clawing for a handhold where there was none, he slipped over the edge and plunged to the ground, screaming.

Trego didn't even wait to recover his rattles. He went down the ladder much faster than he had come up. Running out the front door, he found Furtak just a few feet from the belfry, his head twisted to one side. Trego could see that he had landed on his head and broken his neck. His rifle lay a few feet from him at the edge of the street.

Within a few minutes, there was a crowd at the church. With no coroner in town, Dibble took it on himself to pronounce Furtak dead of a broken neck. He sent men out into the cemetery near town to dig a grave.

Petrauk came into the crowd from across the street, keeping a wary eye on Yonnie

Guzek who had come out with the others. She didn't have her rifle with her.

"I'm arresting the preacher," Petrauk shouted, "for killing Furtak. He pushed him out of the church belfry."

"Give me one good reason why Furtak was up there?" Bridgewood demanded.

"Why he was up there has no bearing on this," Petrauk said. "Trego pushed him out and he was killed."

"You murdering sidewinder!" Yonnie Guzek shouted. "You know that's a lie! I saw the whole thing. Furtak fell out of there by himself before the preacher even got up there."

"She's right," Bridgewood put in. "I saw it, too. Furtak was not pushed. He just fell out of the belfry."

Other heads nodded. Petrauk saw that he was outnumbered and began to back off. Yonnie got in the last word.

"You're just lucky he don't push you off some canyon wall. You deserve it."

Oscar Coy arrived in Genesis just before noon. He was alone. Yonnie and Trego met him in the street.

"Where's the doc?" Yonnie demanded.

"I was bringing him," Coy said. "Then some masked man met us a couple of miles out of town and told the doc to go back. I tried to make him come on, but he wouldn't do it."

"I guess you can't blame him," Trego said. "Did you recognize the masked man?"

Coy shook his head. "Not for sure. But I think it was Grumpy Rush. He sure wouldn't want the doc to come. He'd like to see Quint die so he and Petrauk could take over the whole ranch."

"They ain't going to take over, no matter what happens to Quint," Yonnie said. "I'll bury them both."

Furtak's funeral after noon was a short affair. Trego made the sermon as brief as possible, emphasizing the uncertainties of life and the need to have a hope beyond the grave.

After the funeral, several of the people stopped by to see Quint. He was able to talk to his visitors, and there was little doubt in anyone's mind that he was going to recover even without a doctor's care.

Sunday morning came and the church was crowded. Trego didn't know whether it was because of the basket dinner at noon or whether everyone had suddenly become aware of the church and its preacher and the events of yesterday.

Trego based his sermon on Israel being held captive. He watched certain faces in the crowd to see if they would reveal any sign of nervousness. Trego made the comparison clear between Israel being occupied by enemy soldiers and Genesis being terrorized by the Winchester Gang. He saw no signs of guilt anywhere in the congregation.

When the service was over, Trego stood at the door to shake hands with the people. Vona stopped as she went out.

"What were you trying to prove this morning?" she said nervously. "If any member of the Winchester Gang was in the audience, he'd be sure to take offense at what you said."

"I expected him to," Trego said. "In fact, I wanted him to. I thought I would be able to see it in his face. There are some members of that gang who haven't been smoked out yet, I'm sure. I've got to find out who they are."

"This was hardly the place to smoke them out," Vona said.

Trego didn't want to get into an argument with Vona now. "I thought it would be the ideal place. He wouldn't want to reveal himself to everyone so he'd scowl and fume to himself till the service was over. By then I'd know who he was. But I didn't see anybody even nervous."

Vona suddenly smiled. "Then maybe there

weren't any Winchester men here. We'd like to have you eat with us at the picnic."

Trego grinned. "That sounds like heavenly music to me."

Vona blushed. "Mr. Trego! Don't be sacrilegious right here at church."

Trego looked around. People were visiting all around, but none were close at the moment. "Is it sacrilegious to want to be close to you?" he said softly.

Her blush deepened and she turned away quickly. "Pa says you may ride down to the grounds with us."

"Thank you," he said. He felt like a school boy asking to carry the books of some pig-tailed girl.

He turned from Vona when he saw the Oylers coming toward him. Cal Oyler shook hands quickly and moved on with his wife. Alvena lingered a minute.

"From the looks of Vona, I'd guess that for today you've been spoken for," she said softly, but her words had a sharp edge.

"She invited me to eat with them at the picnic," Trego said. "I didn't want to eat alone."

She looked straight at him. "You wouldn't have."

She moved on and Trego greeted others who wanted to speak to him before heading for the picnic.

The picnic area was down in Ash Creek Canyon, less than half a mile from town but it was quite a drop down to the bottom of the canyon. Trego took what he had prepared for dinner, which was mostly a tin plate and fork and spoon for eating, and put them in Ekhart's wagon.

Tom Ekhart led the wagons down the road into the canyon, then swung off into a grove of cottonwoods a short distance from the road. It was a pretty site and Trego anticipated a relaxing, enjoyable day.

Ekhart announced before they began eating that the business meeting of the church would take place immediately after the picnic baskets were put away. Then there would be some games for the young people and time for the older ones to visit.

Trego had to forego the games because some of the men wanted to talk to him after the business meeting. The vote to offer Trego a permanent job as minister had been overwhelmingly in favor.

Trego tried to keep his mind on what the men were saying, agreeing to the wage they offered with the understanding that he'd have to find some kind of job through the week to make ends meet. His eyes were following the young people in their games, especially Vona. Ordinarily, he considered himself too old to want to participate in games. But today he wanted to be out there as much as any school boy.

When the discussion with the church business was over, Tom Ekhart, Ivan Bridgewood, and Pace Holcomb gathered around Trego to talk in low tones about the Winchester Gang. Trego glanced again at the games and saw that the older group, including some young wives, had broken up their game. Vona was gone. Then he saw her with Katie Holcomb, Pace's wife, going up the canyon. It was a good day for a short hike.

He turned his attention back to the three men and he realized they were pumping him for any new information he had gathered. Briefly, he repeated what he knew about the graves Grumpy Rush had shown him. He was sure Pace had told the others about that. He admitted that he hadn't located the gang leader yet. He watched the others closely as he said that he was suspicious of Cal Oyler.

Bridgewood showed the most surprise, but none of the three argued with him when he explained about the letter and reminded them of the fact that no messages got out or in. Someone had to be tampering with the mail: Oyler was the logical one. Adalbert apparently was involved in the gang, too, since he'd been one of those trying to kill Trego the other night. Adalbert was a good friend of Oyler. He'd been at supper at Oyler's the night Trego was there.

Suddenly a wild yell, almost a hysterical scream, echoed down the canyon. Pace leaped up.

"That's Katie!" he said, and started running.

Trego went after him, catching him within a few yards. He saw Katie running toward the picnic grounds, her hair flying where the pins had given way.

"What's the matter?" Pace yelled when he was close enough to make her hear.

Trego passed Pace when he saw that Vona was not with Katie. They had gone up the canyon together.

"Some masked men!" Katie panted, reaching Trego first. "They took Vona."

# 16

Trego looked up the canyon and started away on a run. Katie stopped him.

"Wait a minute, Sam. It's a trap." She tried to catch her breath. "One of the men said he knew you'd come after Vona."

"How many men were there?" Trego asked.

"Two. I couldn't tell who they were. One was tall and the other one was built like the deputy."

Trego nodded. "Petrauk. He wants a shot at me."

"He said if you didn't come after her, she'd be hurt," Katie said.

"I won't disappoint him," Trego said. "Where was he taking her?"

"I don't know. They went on up the canyon."

Trego started again. Pace came after him.

"You can't go alone," Pace shouted.

"I'd better. It's not you he's after. Petrauk

knows I'm close to pinning those murders on him."

"All the more reason I should go along. Tom will want to come, too. Vona's his daughter."

Trego stopped. "You heard what Katie said. If I don't go after her, she'll be hurt. If you or Tom go along, no telling what he might do to Vona."

"If you go alone, he'll kill you. You can bet he's got it figured so he gets a clear shot at you before you know where he is."

"Likely," Trego said. "But that doesn't change anything. If he does kill me, he'll probably turn Vona loose, unhurt."

"You're too bull-headed to be a preacher," Pace said angrily.

"Also too good with a gun," Trego said. "I don't want to kill anyone, but if there's no other way to get Vona free, then that's how it will be."

Tom Ekhart came up, puffing. Trego jerked a thumb at him. "Keep him here, Pace. It's the only way Vona will be safe."

Trego started on at a long lope. Maybe he could catch Petrauk and whoever was with him. He knew they had a big head start. His eyes raced ahead wherever he could see through the trees along the creek where he was running. He supposed the kidnappers would take Vona straight up the canyon. Then his eyes caught a flash of blue up near the canyon rim. He stopped dead in his tracks. Vona was wearing blue today.

He stared hard at the bluff. Again he saw the blue, and this time he recognized Vona in her blue dress. She was in the mouth of the cave that was just under the rim of the canyon behind the bank. His mind was racing. Petrauk had deliberately allowed Vona to be seen at the mouth of the cave because he wanted Trego to know where she was. From there, he'd have a perfect shot at Trego as he climbed the winding trail up the side of the canyon.

If Petrauk had written out his plan and handed it to Trego, it wouldn't have been clearer. It wasn't Vona he wanted; it was Trego. He must have seen them outside the church this morning and read the signs as clearly as Alvena had. He had set his trap for Trego with irresistible bait.

Trego wasn't quite ready to sacrifice himself needlessly, though. Petrauk might decide to keep Vona now that he had her, even if he killed Trego. Trego had to stay alive.

His eyes searched the canyon wall. A short distance up the dim trail that led to the cave, a gully cut up the face of the wall. It looked to Trego like it notched the canyon rim behind the town hall. He might not be able to climb up that crack, but the attempt would be better than walking blindly into Petrauk's trap by following the path. He crossed the valley floor on the run, aiming directly toward the path. He knew Petrauk would be watching. He wanted him to think he was coming right up that path toward him.

He started up the path at a slower rate. He'd need his strength for the climb up that gully, if he could make it at all. The path dipped out of sight of the cave as it crossed the gully. Trego turned up the gully, finding the going less difficult than he had expected. Still, it wasn't easy climbing and he had to hurry. Petrauk would get suspicious if he didn't show up on the path in a little while.

Near the top of the wall, the gully was steeper and he had to scramble for a foothold to pull himself up to the top. He was exhausted when he sprawled on the ground behind the town hall. Sucking in huge gulps of fresh air, he got to his feet and ran along the rim of the canyon wall to the path leading down to the bench that supported the cave. If Petrauk hadn't gotten suspicious, he'd be waiting just inside the cave for him to show up.

At the corner of the cave, he stopped. He didn't hear anything inside, but he knew they weren't likely to leave this trap they had set. There was a dark pocket back in the wall of the cave just across from him. Drawing a deep breath, he plunged across the opening and inside the cave, aiming for that dark hole. Two shots echoed in the cave, but only dirt exploded in his face as he hit the ground and rolled into the depression. The two men had been watching for him, but they hadn't been prepared for such a sudden appearance.

Trego fired toward the flashes, aiming high so he wouldn't hit Vona. The bullet hit the ceiling and sent rock splinters clattering to the floor. Trego heard sounds retreating deeper into the cave and he ventured out of his hole and dived across the cave against the far wall. Another shot was fired, but it didn't come close. The shot had come from much farther back in the cave. The men were retreating. Ducking low, Trego followed.

Another shot came his way from even deeper in the cave. Trego dodged ahead faster. Suddenly he stopped as he heard a moan close by. Flattening himself against the cave wall, he studied the spot where he'd heard the sound. As his eyes adjusted to the deeper gloom in the cave, he saw something blue. Stooping low, he ran forward.

He found Vona flattened against the cave floor, trembling. "Are you hurt?" he asked softly.

"No," she said. "Just scared. Please take me out of here."

"Why did they leave you?"

"They were scared."

Trego realized they'd left Vona, hoping he'd go back now with her and let them alone. He had them trapped, but the odds were still against him if he followed them. They'd be in the darkness of the cave and, if there was any light coming from the opening, he'd be silhouetted against it.

His real reason for coming this far had been to rescue Vona. He had her now. But the thing that really changed his mind was her plea to be taken out of the cave. Something welled up in his throat that drowned out all other emotions. He no longer cared what happened to those kidnappers. He wanted to get Vona to safety. He scooped her up in his arms, amazed at how light she was. Hugging the side of the cave, he moved back toward the opening. He didn't know how far back into the cave the men had gone, but he hoped it was far enough they wouldn't see them leave.

"Put me down, Mr. Trego," Vona said softly. "I can walk."

He remembered then that she had said she was all right. He was exposing them both to danger by carrying her. Setting her on her feet, he put her ahead of him so he could shield her as they went out of the cave. He expected some shots, but none came.

Once outside, Trego stepped away from the cave then stopped. "Let's straighten out one thing," he said. "I'm not Mr. Trego. I'm Sam."

She nodded, a faint smile on her lips. "All right. Thank you, Sam, for coming after me."

"Who were those two?"

"I couldn't see their faces. But I'm sure the heavy one was Fred Petrauk. I think the tall one was Buck Adalbert."

Pace Holcomb and Tom Ekhart came puffing up the path. "What happened to those two kidnappers?"

"They're trapped in the cave," Trego said. "Pace, will you watch the opening to make sure they don't get out? I'm going to get a light and maybe some more men, or we'll smoke them out."

Pace agreed and Tom Ekhart stayed with

him. Trego took Vona back to the picnic area and found Dibble, suggesting that they get a lantern up in town and look for the men in the cave.

"You got Vona back safely," Dibble said. "I think we'd better let well enough alone."

"Men like those two have to be taught that they can't run roughshod over the whole community," Trego said.

"You think shooting them will teach them anything?"

"I was thinking of taking them down to Sage City and letting the sheriff throw them in jail till they're tried for kidnapping," Trego said. "But we've got to catch them first."

Reluctantly, Dibble agreed but he wasn't in favor of getting into a gun battle if it could be avoided.

"We'll have to have a light," Trego said. "Can you find a lantern?"

Dibble nodded. "I have one in my store. But if we carry a lantern down into that cave, we'll make a perfect target of ourselves. How about hanging the lantern on the end of a long pole? When they see the light, they might start shooting at that. We'll know then where they are."

"Good idea," Trego agreed.

Katie Holcomb drove them up the steep

road to town in the Holcomb spring wagon. Dibble got a lantern from his store while Trego found a long pole behind the building. After tying the lantern to the end of the pole, they made their way on foot down the path behind the bank.

They lit the lantern and Trego carried the pole, holding the lantern as far from him as possible. Pace and Tom Ekhart followed the two into the cave. As they advanced, Trego saw the fresh dirt piled along the sides of the cave. It puzzled him but he put it out of his mind, concentrating on what he'd do when they found the two men. They must be hiding at the very end of the cave.

There were no sounds ahead, and then they came to the place where the floor slanted sharply upward. Fresh dirt was over all the floor here. It had obviously been dug out of the tunnel in front of them.

"Someone's been making this cave bigger," Tom Ekhart said. "Why?"

"I heard that this cave was used by horse thieves once," Dibble said. "Maybe they did it."

Trego didn't argue. He'd heard the horse thief story, too. But this dirt looked like it had been freshly dug.

"There's nobody in here," Dibble said. "They must have found some side tunnel and got out another way."

Trego recalled small tunnels running off from the main tunnel back near the mouth, but he hadn't thought they were big enough for a man to go through. Still, there didn't seem to be any other explanation. The lantern showed the tunnel ahead sloping sharply upward until it appeared to run into the ceiling a few yards away.

"Looks that way," Trego admitted grudgingly. He'd have felt better if he could have seen Petrauk and Adalbert in the jail at Sage City.

On the way out of the cave, Trego looked at the little side tunnels. He didn't see any that appeared to lead anywhere. Back at the picnic area, the people had gathered things up and were only waiting for the men to return to head for home.

The Ekharts had brought Trego down from town, but Katie offered to take him back. "We want to visit Quint Guzek, anyway," she said.

Trego helped Vona into the Ekhart wagon. "You be careful," she said softly.

He nodded, thinking that those words were sound advice. If Petrauk would resort to a trick like he'd used today to get to him, he'd not be above taking advantage of any opportunity to kill him. As the Holcomb spring wagon started up the steep road to the town level, Katie turned to Trego who was standing behind the spring seat.

"I doubt if Quint Guzek would be thrilled out of his boots by a visit from homesteaders like us," she said. "I asked to bring you back to town, Sam, because I wanted to talk to you alone. Pace told me about you finding his pa's grave. Do you have any idea who is doing the killing?"

"I've got an idea, all right," Trego said, "but no proof. Zeb Myrick identified Furtak's voice as one he heard when he was robbed. He said one was a tall man; the other one short. Rush and Skeen were eliminated. So if Furtak was the tall one, then it seems logical that Petrauk was the short one."

Pace nodded in agreement. "The way things turned out today, maybe it's a good thing that Web and Uldine decided to stay with Zeb instead of bringing him to the picnic. Petrauk might have found a way to kill him."

"Whoever is the brains behind this outfit has collected a lot of money," Trego said thoughtfully. "He's got seven thousand dollars they took from Uncle Luther. I fully intend to get that back. But who is the brains? Could it be Cal Oyler?"

"I've suspected Cal of doing some crooked things," Pace said, "but I can't believe he'd stoop to murder. Maybe it's Petrauk."

"I don't think Petrauk is smart enough to mastermind this scheme," Trego said.

"It has to be somebody who has a lot of money now," Pace said. "No telling how many people they have lured in here with all their life's savings. There's just nobody in town who seems to have a lot of money except the banker."

"I can't believe it is Bridgewood," Trego said. "Whoever it is must be hiding the money somewhere. If he started spending a lot, people would suspect him of getting it illegally."

Pace and Katie let Trego off at the parsonage, not even stopping to go in to see Quint Guzek. Trego was getting used to having Quint and Yonnie in the big guest bedroom in the parsonage. Yonnie did most of the cooking for all three of them and Trego appreciated that.

Today as he went in, Yonnie called him back to the big bedroom. Trego had planned to go to the far end of the house to the room he called his office.

"Something wrong?" he asked.

"Somebody was in the house this afternoon," Quint said from the bed where he was propped up on pillows. "We heard him prowling around. Yonnie was going to go see who it was, but I wouldn't let her. He might have killed her."

Trego nodded. "You were right. I'll go see what happened."

The minute he stepped into the room where he prepared his sermons, he saw the mess. Somebody had literally torn the place apart. They must have been looking for something that the previous preacher, Knowles, had left. Was it that list of the members of the Winchester Gang that Trego was sure was around here somewhere?

Was the intruder still here? Maybe he was lingering around, waiting for a chance to get rid of the current preacher.

# 17

Trego cautiously went over that entire end of the house. Whoever had been here was gone now. As he picked up the papers and boxes strewn around, he looked for some clue that would tell him what the burglar had been looking for.

He thought of the paper he'd found stuck on the back of the desk. The thief hadn't gotten that because Trego had put it in his bible and he'd left that at the church. His mind went back to the man behind these killings. That man must have a lot of money put away somewhere. The logical place was the bank. He'd check as soon as Bridgewood opened up tomorrow morning.

It wouldn't be long until Guzek could be moved back to his home. He was improving rapidly. It had been a clean wound and apparently had hit nothing vital. Guzek was a hard, tough man, anyway. Now he was chomping at the bit to get back on the ranch before Petrauk moved in and took possession.

As soon as breakfast was over Monday morning, Trego went outside, checking the deputy's office. It was open warfare between him and Petrauk now. Petrauk was making no attempt to hide his hate for Trego, and his attempts to kill him were only thinly camouflaged.

The deputy was not in his office and Trego wandered over town, stopping to visit a while with Dibble, then dropping in at the store to talk to Oyler, trying to decide if his suspicions of the storekeeper had any real grounds. Oyler was aloof but not really unfriendly.

When the bank opened across the street from the store, Trego made his way over there.

"Is there anybody depositing unusual amounts of money in the bank?" he asked Bridgewood.

Bridgewood shrugged his shoulders. "I don't see much money coming in or going out of the bank," he said. "I've been wondering if I was wrong in opening a bank here. There are no other banks anywhere near so it seemed like a smart thing to do. I was sure I'd get all the business for miles around."

"Don't you?"

"If I do, there just isn't as much business as I thought there would be."

"Who has the biggest accounts here?" Trego asked.

Bridgewood's eyebrows shot up. "I can't tell you that. That's private information. Why do you want to know?"

"Several men have been killed coming to Genesis," Trego said. "Everyone of them was robbed; or at least, it appears that way. I want to know where that money is."

"I'm sure it isn't in my bank," Bridgewood said. "The biggest accounts I have are for the stores in town. They have to have capital to buy their goods and, of course, they keep their receipts here in the bank."

Trego thought of Oyler again. "Those accounts are not unusually big?"

Bridgewood shook his head. "Barely enough to keep them going."

"Evidence points to Furtak being one of those who did the killing. He didn't have a large account?"

Bridgewood frowned. "Again, that's none of your business," he said. "But I will tell you that he didn't have enough to buy a new anvil."

"Petrauk?" Trego pressed.

"Same," Bridgewood said.

"Then you're sure the money being stolen by this gang is not getting to your bank?"

Bridgewood shook his head. "I wish some more money would come in. I could make more loans right now if I had the money."

Trego rubbed his chin. "Thanks for the help, Mr. Bridgewood."

He went down to the livery barn, keeping an eye out for Petrauk. Getting his horse, he rode across Ash Creek Canyon to Tom Ekhart's place. Ekhart was in the field and Trego rode out there.

"I've been doing some thinking," he said when Ekhart stopped his team and came over to Trego's horse. "Who do you think will be hit next by this gang of extortionists?"

"I've been thinking about that, too," Ekhart said. "They've hit the Holcombs, the Greens, and the Myricks. All are close neighbors of mine."

"You're about the only one in this area who hasn't been hit," Trego said.

"Maybe I'm lucky. But I think there is a good reason. Everyone who has been hit — like Pace and Katie — had some relative back where they came from who had some money. Whoever is doing this is doing a lot of nosing around. They know who's got the money before they set their trap. Now I don't have any relatives with money. In fact, I've got more money myself than anybody back home. So they wouldn't make much by reporting to them that I'd been kidnapped."

"That makes sense," Trego said. "But a greedy bunch of cutthroats like this can be depended on to get everything available. If they know who has the money back where people come from, they probably know who has the money here, too."

Tom nodded. "Meaning they'll try to get my money, too? I've thought of that. So I put all my money in the bank."

Trego's mind was racing, trying to imagine he was the mastermind of this gang. What would he do? The answer was so clear, it left no doubt in Trego's mind. That bank would be robbed. What better way to complete the collection of all the portable wealth in the country?

"Ever thought that the bank might be robbed?" he asked.

Tom nodded. "Yes, I've thought of that, too. Since I've found out what is going on, there aren't many things I haven't thought about. But Bridgewood has a strong vault with thick walls and a good lock. My money is safer there than here at home."

"That's probably right," Trego agreed.

"I'm going to keep an eye open for anyone paying particular attention to the bank. It would really help if we knew who to watch."

Vona came out of the house as Trego rode back through the yard. "Katie was over and said that Yonnie expects to take Quint home tomorrow," she said. "So we're planning to clean the parsonage on Wednesday if you have no objection."

Trego had thought of the job he'd be facing in washing bedding and giving the parsonage a general cleaning. He knew that would be expected after Quint and Yonnie Guzek had been there for several days. He hadn't considered the possibility that the women of the church would come in and do it.

"If you expect me to object to that, you're badly mistaken," he said with a grin. "I'll carry water or swing a mop to help. But I'll be mighty grateful to have somebody in charge who knows what she's doing."

"We'll be there about eight Wednesday morning," Vona said.

Trego hadn't known that Yonnie and Quint expected to go home tomorrow. Yonnie had not spoken to him any more than necessary since his sermon on gossip, even when she was staying in his house. He didn't blame her, and he welcomed the privilege of not having to listen to her gossip.

On Tuesday morning Quint Guzek wasn't feeling able to make the trip home, so Trego suggested they stay another day. They could leave Wednesday morning before the ladies came to clean if they wanted to. Trego stayed in town on Tuesday. Here was the place where things were going to happen, he felt. He checked the bank, and agreed with Tom Ekhart that the vault there appeared completely safe from any robber except one with dynamite.

Wednesday morning, Yonnie decided to stay and help the women clean the parsonage. She said she helped make the mess; she'd help clean it up. Quint was moved to a makeshift bed on a cot. Oscar Coy came to town early in the big wagon with a bed made in the back. Now he was faced with a day in town with nothing to do. Yonnie's decisions were not to be challenged.

By half past eight, the parsonage was full of women. Vona and Martha Ekhart, Uldine Myrick, Katie Holcomb, Alvena and Neleda Oyler, along with several other women, were there. Trego learned from Uldine that Web Myrick was keeping a close guard on his brother, Zeb. According to Alvena, Cal Oyler wasn't too happy about being left with the store to handle by himself. When the work began, Edna Bridgewood came over from her house to help.

Trego's offer to help was rejected. Today's work was women's work and a man just got in the way. Horace Dibble came down from the drugstore to see what he could do to help and, when he found that the women had brought lunches, he offered to make lemonade and bring it down at noon. That offer was eagerly accepted.

It was about the middle of the forenoon when Vona came outside looking for Trego. It seemed to Trego that the house was a total shambles, punctuated by mop buckets, dust rags, tubs of soaking sheets and blankets, clothes stompers, and washboards.

"This fell out of a book I was dusting," Vona said. She handed him a paper. "It had been stuck there, but came loose. It looks like a sermon outline. Doesn't make much sense to me. I thought it might to you."

Trego glanced at it and shook his head. "Must have been Knowles' sermon. But why would he hide it in a book?"

"I'll let you figure that out," Vona said. "I've got to get back to the cleaning."

Trego took the paper over to the church where the breeze wouldn't flutter it around. He stood at the pulpit and read it carefully. He agreed with Vona. It did look like a sermon outline. The heading was: "Thou Shalt Not Kill — Exodus 20:13."

Under the heading were a few notes about killing:

A strong man kills with strength.
A coward kills by trickery.
A vicious man kills by torture.
A deceitful man kills by cunning (poison).
A rich man hires his killing done.

Trego stared at the paper. What kind of a sermon could a minister preach from that outline? There was nothing there about the sin of killing, except the text, "Thou shalt not kill." What had Knowles meant? Suddenly he thought of Knowles' search for the identity of the members of the Winchester Gang. Maybe this sermon was aimed directly at the members of the gang.

Could each note he had made refer to one of them? He went over the notes again. The strong man could very well have been Jumbo Furtak — or possibly Grumpy Rush. Who was the coward? It took him only a second to decide that would have been Dett Skeen. He had always hidden behind Grumpy Rush. But he was a killer, if he got the opportunity to kill without running much personal risk.

Trego's eyes dropped down to the next line, the vicious man, the one who killed by torture. Among those that Trego had identified to his own satisfaction as being members of the gang, Fred Petrauk would come nearest fitting the description of a vicious man. Trego had no trouble picturing him as a man who could torture any enemy and enjoy it.

Trego was stumped on the next one, the deceitful man. That word in parentheses at the end, poison, jumped at Trego. He hadn't heard of anybody being poisoned. Of course, he didn't know how all those men in the graves out in the canyon had died. Maybe they had been poisoned, but he doubted it. He was guessing they had been robbed and deliberately shot.

The only other men that Trego suspected of being in the gang were Buck Adalbert and possibly Cal Oyler, although he got little support from anyone in his suspicion of Oyler. Trego couldn't imagine either of those men resorting to poison. But then, what kind of a man did it take to use poison to kill?

And who was the rich man who hired his killing done? That was the one Trego really wanted to find. The rich man, if he was involved in the Winchester Gang, would certainly be the one who was holding the stolen money. He was probably the leader of the gang and ordered the killings carried out by those who worked for him. He'd be the one who had Trego's five thousand dollars. Trego had better find out who it was mighty soon, or he probably wouldn't live to recover his money.

He believed this was the outline of a sermon, maybe the last one that Knowles preached. He wondered if Knowles had lived long enough to preach it. If he had, that had very likely led directly to his death. He hadn't been killed by the man who used poison. Maybe it had been the coward who used trickery. Trego couldn't imagine what trick could have been used to make a team run off a canyon rim.

It sounded more like the man who used strength. A strong man could force a running team to the edge of a canyon wall and the law of gravity would take care of the rest.

Who was the rich man? The only man here in Genesis whom Trego considered rich was Ivan Bridgewood. Trego rejected that possibility. If he was the gang leader, then he qualified as the deceitful man, too. It was unthinkable to suspect Bridgewood. Trego was interrupted in his thoughts by

Oscar Coy coming in the back door of the church.

"Vona said she thought you were over here," he said. "I hate to interrupt you in your work on your sermon, but I wanted to talk to you."

"I'm not working on my sermon," Trego said, sliding the paper under the Bible. He'd come back to that later and try to reach some conclusions. "What's on your mind?"

"I wanted to tell you something I heard when I was in Sage Creek to get the doc for Quint."

Trego went back to the chair behind the pulpit and sat down. Coy stepped up on the edge of the podium.

"I went to the sheriff there," he said. "I told him what Petrauk and Rush had done, but he wouldn't believe me. He told me something that I didn't believe, either, but it stuck in my mind. He asked if I knew any odd characters up here. I told him the oddest one we had was the one he'd put up here as a deputy.

"He said he had an old dodger there that he'd run across. It was several years old. It was a wanted poster for a killer who used poison to kill. He had another letter dated only a couple of years ago that said it was thought that this killer had come to these canyons. The sheriff figured he might be in Genesis, since this is on the raw edge of everything so far as the law is concerned."

Trego's eyes shifted to the pulpit where Knowles' sermon outline lay under the Bible. The deceitful man who killed by cunning (poison). Was he here in Genesis? Trego was guessing he had been here when Knowles outlined that sermon. And the chances were good that he was still here.

## 18

Trego got up and he and Coy went outside. Trego looked down the one street in the bright light of the noon sun.

"Do you have any idea who it might be?" he asked Coy.

Coy shook his head. "It sounded crazy to me when the sheriff suggested that he might be in Genesis. Then I got to thinking of all the murders here and I wondered if he might be right. I told the sheriff about those graves and he said he'd look into it, but he didn't sound very enthusiastic."

"Sometimes we have to solve our own problems," Trego said.

Katie came to the parsonage door and called to them. "We're going to eat now."

"Sounds good, Katie," Trego said. "I'll go down to Dibble's and get the lemonade."

Trego hurried down the street. He found Dibble just inside the drugstore with a bucket full of lemonade. He also had a small pitcher of it.

"I had a little more made than would go in the bucket," Dibble explained, "so I put it in this pitcher for you. Thought you might not be eating with the others, anyway."

"It looks mighty good," Trego said. "The ladies will be tickled to see this. They've been working hard this morning."

"This is the least I can do," Dibble said. "I like to see the church work go forward. And it's a cinch they wouldn't let me get under foot trying to help them with the cleaning."

"You're right about that," Trego said. "I got shoved out."

Trego started back to the church and his mind returned to what he and Coy had been talking about. He couldn't get it off his mind about the coincidence of finding Knowles' sermon notes at the same time that Coy reported on the man who poisoned his victims. The only incongruous thing was that nobody killed around Genesis had been poisoned so far as Trego knew. Actually, a man disappearing into these canyons years ago could be anywhere in the world by now.

He delivered the bucket of lemonade to the women and listened to their chorus of approval. He took some of the sandwiches the women had brought and his pitcher of lemonade, and went outside to sit on the steps. Alvena Oyler came out to sit with him.

His mind kept returning to the man who killed with poison. He wasn't likely to be in Genesis now. But what if he was? He'd be deceitful, according to Knowles' notes, so he could be anyone. Even the banker or the druggist. That thought hit Trego hard. Dibble was one of the best friends he had here. But who would have a better opportunity to poison people than a druggist with all those drugs and poisons at his fingertips?

He looked at his individual pitcher of lemonade. Was it different from that in the bucket? The odds were a hundred to one that it wasn't. But that one chance in a hundred could kill. He got up and handed his plate of sandwiches to Alvena.

"Will you take them back inside for me? I need to see Dibble for a minute. I'll be right back."

He waited until Alvena had carried his sandwiches back inside. Then he took the pitcher of lemonade around the corner of the house and set it down where no one would drink from it. Then he hurried up the street to the drugstore.

"Wasn't the lemonade good?" Dibble asked in alarm.

"Perfect," Trego said. "They were very thirsty. They really went after it. Alvena even took my pitcher full."

Dibble's eyes widened momentarily then came back to normal. Trego was watching him closely. "Do you need more?" Dibble asked.

"I reckon we can use a little more," Trego said. "At least, I can. I haven't had any yet."

"I'll bring some down right away," he said.

Trego wished he could stay and see Dibble mix it up but there was no excuse for staying longer. He went back to the parsonage, doubting if he'd done anything except gotten himself in trouble because Dibble would wonder why Trego had lied if he discovered that the lemonade wasn't all gone.

He stopped at the corner of the house to get his pitcher of lemonade. He found the pitcher upset and the lemonade all gone. Sitting by contentedly licking his chops was the big white bulldog of Dibble's. Trego remembered then that he hadn't seen him at the store. The dog apparently had been attracted by all the people at the parsonage and had come down here. Trego really would need more lemonade now.

Stepping inside, he found the bucket of lemonade practically empty. He knew that it would be gone by the time Dibble got here with more. He got his sandwiches and ate them.

By the time he had finished, Dibble had arrived with more lemonade. He looked over the crowd and Trego thought he looked relieved when he saw Alvena. It was just his imagination, he supposed, because he knew how much Dibble thought of Alvena.

Dibble went back outside and walked around the church. When he went back up the street, Trego thought he looked paler than usual and his step was quick as if he'd seen a ghost. Trego went around the church to see what he'd found. At the corner, he stopped short. There was the big white bulldog stretched out, gasping his last.

Trego's first thought was that the lemonade meant for him had been poisoned and the dog had gotten it instead. He wanted to reject that. Dibble was his friend; he had sided with him in almost everything. But Knowles' notes haunted him. "A deceitful man kills by cunning (poison)." A deceitful man could pretend to be a friend when he was really an enemy.

Shaken, Trego went back to the house and picked up the lemonade that Dibble had brought. He hadn't poisoned the drink for the women; he likely hadn't poisoned this. But Trego was taking no chances.

"Maybe you should take that back to Mr. Dibble," Vona said. "We've had all we want. Thank him again for us."

Still shaken, still doubting that Dibble had really tried to poison him, Trego took the bucket of lemonade back to the drugstore.

"The ladies had all they wanted," Trego said easily. "They said to thank you again. It really refreshed them."

"Glad I could do something to help," Dibble said, barely glancing up from the ledger he was writing in.

Trego looked at Dibble with new eyes, trying to picture him as a man who would poison someone. It was hard to do after considering him one of his truest friends. But the doubts were overwhelming.

He set the bucket down and went back outside. This still didn't tell Trego where the stolen money was. Maybe Dibble was the gang leader. If so, where was he hiding the money? Maybe he had another account in the bank, one that didn't have his name on it at all.

Crossing the street, he went up to the bank. Ivan Bridgewood watched him come to the window.

"I'm not asking for names this time," Trego said. "But I need to know if you have any organizational accounts that are big. Or any big accounts from out of town."

Bridgewood shook his head. "You are a nosey preacher. So was Knowles. And you know what happened to him. Be careful. I can't reveal personal information but I can tell you there are no unusual or extra large accounts in the bank."

Trego nodded. If Bridgewood was telling the truth, it was obvious that the stolen money wasn't in the bank. From what Bridgewood said, probably the only big accounts were those of the storekeepers and Tom Ekhart. Anyone else who had a little money likely had it here. Bridgewood himself must have everything he had in here or out on loan.

If the money brought into the area for ransom had not been deposited in the bank, then the ones who stole it might very well be planning to rob the bank itself. Most of the money left in the country was likely here.

Trego left the bank and hurried back to the parsonage, a new idea brewing in his mind. He found Oscar Coy sitting against the parsonage wall.

"Hardest work I've done today," Coy grinned as Trego squatted beside him. "Letting my dinner settle."

"What do you know about the cave west

of the bank?" Trego asked.

"It's been there forever so far as I know," Coy said. "They say that horse thieves once used it as a hideout. I've been in it several times."

"How about going once more?" Trego said.

"Didn't know you were kid enough to want to explore caves. But I'll show it to you. Get a lantern."

Trego and Coy made their way to the path behind the bank that led down to the mouth of the cave. Trego had a stick and a lantern. Before they had gone fifty feet into the cave, Coy pointed to the fresh dirt.

"Somebody's been digging. This cave's only about fifty yards deep."

"It was," Trego corrected. "I want you to tell me what you think of the end of this cave now. I saw it Sunday when we came looking for the men who grabbed Vona Ekhart."

Coy sputtered when he saw the dirt strung along the sides and piled at what used to be the end of the cave. Trego went on up the steep incline of the newly excavated tunnel. He tapped his stick against the roof until he was rewarded by a hollow sound.

"Some building right above here," he said.

"Is somebody trying to drop the whole

241

town into this cave?" Coy sputtered.

"I'm guessing we're right under the bank. This cave is just west of the bank, you know. There's more ways to get into a bank than by the front door."

Coy's jaw dropped. "You think somebody is fixing to rob the bank?"

"Can you think of any other reason for digging this tunnel beyond the end of the cave?"

"But the tunnel goes on," Coy said. "Why would they dig any farther?"

"That's one thing I want to find out. Let's go on."

The tunnel got smaller with every foot. Trego was down on his knees crawling before he had gone very far. The tunnel ahead looked to be about the same size, and Trego thought he glimpsed a piece of wood in the ceiling at the end. A trapdoor, he decided.

He considered going on to that door and making sure he was seeing right. But he vetoed that notion. Likely that trapdoor opened into the drugstore and he didn't want to push it open to find himself staring into the muzzle of a gun. He'd come back tonight and look.

Coy was behind Trego and couldn't see past him. "What's up there?" he asked.

"The end of the tunnel," Trego said. He wouldn't tell Coy that he'd seen what he thought was a trapdoor. Coy might have acquired some of Yonnie's habit of telling too much.

They retreated to the mouth of the cave and climbed back up to the level of the town. When they got to the parsonage, they found that the women had completed their job and Quint and Yonnie Guzek were ready to go home. Coy brought the wagon around to the door and they loaded Quint onto the bed in the wagon and Coy drove out of town.

After thanking the women for the cleaning job, Trego went up to the drugstore. He wanted to find the trapdoor to that tunnel. The more he thought about it, the more logical it seemed that the tunnel must come into the drugstore. Admitting at last that Dibble probably had intended to poison him with that lemonade, it seemed reasonable that Dibble was also the leader of the gang. The tunnel made sense when considered in that light. The gang could meet at Dibble's, go down into the tunnel through the trapdoor, cut a hole into the bank through the floor, rob the bank, and have the money out of the country before Bridgewood discovered it was gone.

No customers were in the store when Trego got there. Dibble welcomed Trego with a big smile. "It's been dull here today. Everybody was working at the parsonage. Need something?"

"Just killing time," Trego said. He looked around. "What happened to your dog?"

Dibble shrugged. "Old age, I guess. He just stretched out and died down by the church."

Trego wandered around, looking for the trapdoor. It wasn't in the main room unless Dibble had it covered up, which was certainly possible. Trego was guessing that it was probably in the back room.

"Anybody in your saloon?" he asked.

"Don't get many customers there," Dibble said. "At least, not till late in the day."

Trego stepped to the door and looked inside. The dog that had always prevented him from snooping around was gone now. No one was in the back room. The tables were ready for the players and the bar at the side stood empty. Trego looked for a door in the floor, but didn't see one. He did see a safe in the far corner and that intrigued him. Maybe that was the place where the stolen money was kept.

"It really is quiet in there today," he said, stepping back and closing the door.

Dibble nodded. "Dett Skeen practically lived in that back room. He always had Grumpy with him. That brought others to play cards with them. So I had some business there most of the time. Since Skeen was killed, nobody comes."

Trego went back outside and moved down the street toward the parsonage. As always when he went down this street, he glanced at the deputy's office. Petrauk hadn't been in that office much since he'd shot Quint Guzek. Trego knew he was around somewhere. Rush was missing, too. He stayed with Petrauk most of the time since Dett Skeen had been killed. They'd probably show up when Trego least wanted to see them, and he was resolved that they wouldn't catch him unprepared.

As soon as it was totally dark, Trego took an unlighted lantern and some matches and made his way to the canyon rim and over the side where no one in town could see him. Reaching the mouth of the cave, he went inside.

Deep into the cave, he stopped and lighted the lantern. The stores were closed now and everybody should be home. He was going to open that trapdoor if he could and see where he was. If he was in Dibble's drugstore, he'd have a try at opening that safe.

The stolen money was probably there. Five thousand dollars of that belonged to him and he intended to get it.

He made good progress through the cave with the aid of the lantern. Reaching the trapdoor after crawling on hands and knees for the last ten yards, he checked the door. From the nails sticking down on one side, he guessed that the door was on leather hinges. Pushing on the other side of the door, he found that it gave a little, then stopped. Something was sitting on the door. He gave it a harder shove and something scraped across the floor above, making a terrible racket. Trego hoped it wasn't that noisy above.

The door opened slowly as the scraping continued. Trego took a chance and poked his head up through the door. It was dark there, and he set the lantern up on the floor. It was then that he saw that he wasn't in Dibble's drugstore. He was in Oyler's general store.

Quickly he climbed up through the door. It was a tight squeeze but it had been made for a big man. Moving the lantern and keeping it low to the floor, he looked around. Almost immediately he noticed the safe that Oyler had against the north wall. Probably Trego had seen it before, but he'd paid no attention to it. Maybe the money was in Oyler's safe.

He had started across to it when he heard a door slam behind the store. That would be at Cal Oyler's house. Quickly Trego blew out the lantern, plunging the store interior into darkness. He was trapped in here and with no explanation for being here when he was caught.

# 19

Listening carefully, Trego heard footsteps outside the back door of the store. Remembering that open trapdoor, he hurried back to it, feeling his way. His eyes were becoming accustomed to the darkness which was relieved only by faint light filtering into the store through the windows.

He heard the steps almost at the back door. He found the trapdoor but he didn't have time to wiggle through the hole so he swung the door shut. A keg sat next to it. That must have been over the door, Trego decided, and shoved it back in place, wincing as it squealed softly when he moved it.

The back door rattled as somebody fit a key into the lock, and Trego dived in behind the counter. At the far end of the counter a bolt of cloth was spread out, the cloth hanging down. Trego got behind the end of the counter, the cloth forming a curtain in front of him.

The door swung open and Cal Oyler came in. He was carrying a lantern. He moved to the center of the room, holding the lantern high. The light fell around Trego and behind him, but the counter kept him in shadow. Alvena Oyler was only a few steps behind her father.

"What do you see, Pa?" she asked.

"Nothing, but I was sure I heard somebody in here," Oyler said.

Trego could peek out and see him. He was looking at the keg sitting on the trapdoor. Trego hadn't moved anything else. Oyler moved slowly around the room, looking carefully at everything. Trego expected him to look behind this counter soon. If he was found, there was no excuse that he could give for being here. He could only guess that Oyler was involved in the gang, he had no proof. This tunnel reaching back to his store didn't prove anything except that somebody had done a lot of digging.

While Oyler walked slowly around the store, holding the lantern high, Alvena pushed the keg over closer to the counter and sat down. Trego could see her, and she didn't even glance at the floor. Obviously she didn't know that trapdoor was there. Cal knew, and his eyes dropped down there then whipped away.

As Oyler prowled around the store, Trego moved in closer under the cascade of cloth from the bolt on the counter. The store-keeper completed his circle back to his daughter.

"You must have been dreaming, Pa," Alvena said. "Let's go back to bed."

"I heard something," Oyler said. "Even after I got out of the house, I heard a noise over here."

"Maybe somebody's cat got in here," Alvena suggested.

"If it did, we'd better find it or we won't have any crackers or cookies fit to sell."

Oyler made another tour of the store. Again he only glanced at the bolt of cloth at the end of the counter. Grumbling, he finally yielded to Alvena's request to go back home.

"I'm going to keep an eye on the store," he said as he went through the door.

Trego was sure that Oyler would be back. If he was involved as Trego was sure now that he was, he couldn't afford to let anyone discover his secret.

As soon as the two were gone, Trego slipped back to the trapdoor and lifted it. He didn't have to move the keg now. Alvena had done that for him. Trego still had the lantern, although it wasn't lit. He didn't dare leave anything behind that would be proof that someone had been here.

Just as he started down through the trap-door, he heard a shuffle outside the store. Oyler must be coming back. Sliding through the opening, he brought the lantern down after him. Then he reached up and swung the door shut. Oyler would remember that Alvena had moved the keg off the door.

As Trego backed down the narrow passageway on his hands and knees, he heard footsteps pounding on the floor above. Only when he got back down the hand-dug tunnel to the original cave where he could stand up did he feel safe.

Once out of the cave, he followed a narrow trail that was a few feet below the lip of the canyon. He wanted to be sure that no one saw him go back home. The trail was dim and not used much, but it led him to the corner of the corral behind the livery barn. From there, Trego made his way across to the blacksmith shop and to the rear door of the parsonage.

He stopped there, his eye on the light in Dibble's house behind his drugstore. The light didn't surprise him. But Trego heard loud voices. That did surprise him.

As suspicious as he was of Dibble now, Trego decided those loud voices must be investigated. Moving behind Bridgewood's house, he cut across the vacant area to the corner of Dibble's house. He recognized Dibble's voice, but the other voice that cut into the druggist's words shocked him. He'd heard that voice only minutes ago. Cal Oyler was arguing with Dibble.

"You came through the cave into my store," Oyler was half shouting. "I heard you in there. Nobody except Petrauk and Rush and you and me know about that tunnel. Petrauk's out at his place. Rush is with him. So it had to be you."

"I haven't left this house tonight," Dibble shot back. "Why would I want to get into your store? You haven't even got much food in there that's fit to eat."

"You've been wanting to hog the show ever since I brought you here," Oyler shouted. "Just remember, if I let the Texas authorities know you're here, you'll be back in prison before you know what's going on. Get that through your bald head."

Trego backed off. Dibble was liable to throw Oyler out of the house any second, and Trego had to be gone. He darted across the open space behind Bridgewood's house to the parsonage and went inside.

There was no longer any doubt that both Oyler and Dibble were involved in something crooked that also included Petrauk and Rush. When Trego had decided that Dibble was the deceitful man that Knowles had listed, he thought that he might also be the rich man who hired his killing done. Now he wondered if Cal Oyler might be the rich one. Obviously Oyler held a club over Dibble with his knowledge that Dibble was dodging the law for something, probably some poison murders in Texas. If Oyler was the real gang leader, then Trego's money very likely was in Oyler's safe.

With their suspicions growing that someone was closing in on them, Oyler and Dibble would likely strike at the bank soon. Trego was jumping to the conclusion that robbing the bank was going to be the gang's final blow to the community. They had siphoned off all the money they could bring into the area with the kidnapping hoax. Anything left that they could grab was in the bank. Trego couldn't believe all that digging had been done for nothing.

Trego was back at the bank the next morning. He went directly to Bridgewood's office.

"I know you've doubted some of the things I've said," Trego began, "but I want you to believe this. This bank is going to be robbed very soon. We may be able to stop it if we work together."

"You're talking crazy, Preacher," Bridgewood said, frowning. "Nobody can break into my safe. I'll just keep it locked at all times, except when I have to get into it."

"They have other ways of getting into the vault."

Bridgewood leaned forward, apparently partly convinced by Trego's sincerity. "They? Are you talking about the Winchester Gang?"

"That's as good a name for them as any."

"Who are they?"

"I'm not sure I know them all. But I know several. Two are dead, Furtak and Dett Skeen. Our deputy, Petrauk, is one and, of course, Rush. The two that I think are the leaders are Cal Oyler and the man I thought was my good friend, Horace Dibble."

Bridgewood's mouth dropped open. "Not Oyler and Dibble," he said softly.

Trego nodded. "I need to know if their money is still in the bank. If they draw it out, that's a sure sign they're ready to strike."

"Why would they draw it out if they plan to steal it, anyway?"

"To keep from having to share their own money with the others in the gang," Trego said. "I've done a lot of thinking since I found out who the leaders are. Do both Oyler and Dibble have their own money in the bank yet?"

Bridgewood's face blanched. "Cal took out most of his money yesterday," he said, his voice almost a whisper. "Said he was going to make a buying trip. This morning, just before you came in, Horace came in and took out most of his. Didn't even give a reason."

"The time is close," Trego said.

"My vault is safe," Bridgewood said confidently. "I had it built burglar-proof. Let me show you."

Trego followed him out of the office to look at the vault. It would be hard to blow it open. Trego searched the floor in the lobby of the bank. He stopped a few feet from the vault.

"Does your vault have a concrete or iron floor?"

Bridgewood shook his head. "That's not necessary. Nobody's going to get into it from below. I made it burglar-proof up here."

"They *are* going to come up from below," Trego said, and explained about the cave. He pointed to the floor. "See that little hole?"

The banker leaned over. "How did that

255

get there? These flooring boards were supposed to be flawless."

"That hole was bored from below, probably some night during the last week. Likely Dibble or Oyler located this hole when he came in to withdraw his money. It doesn't take an expert to see that if they cut about eight feet to the northwest of that little hole, they'll come up inside the vault."

"How will we stop them?" Bridgewood asked excitedly. "They may do it today."

Trego shook his head. "Not today. Tonight probably. You'd hear them if they sawed their way through while you were here. At night, they'll have plenty of time."

"I'll get the deputy," the banker said. "I'll —"

"The deputy will be doing the sawing from below," Trego said. "I'm going to go out and round up some men to help. Maybe we can stop them. Watch for anything suspicious."

Satisfied that the banker was alarmed at last, Trego left the bank and hurried down to the livery stable. He had no real plan in mind, but he knew he had to get one fast. Trego wouldn't lose any money in the bank robbery itself, because he didn't have any in the bank. But either Oyler or Dibble had the money taken from Luther Holcomb. If the gang robbed the bank, it was a good guess that they'd all disappear immediately. If Trego intended to get his money, he had to do it before they got away.

He stopped at Pace's place and explained what he knew, Pace agreed to be in town before sundown. Trego went on to Ekhart's farm and explained the situation. Before Trego left, Oscar Coy stopped in on his way to town. He asked to be counted in. They'd all be in town by sundown.

Trego rode back to town with Coy. Coy had supplies to get for the ranch, but he said he'd get them out to the ranch and be back.

The day dragged for Trego. He discarded half a dozen plans to thwart the bank robbers before deciding that the best way would be to catch them just after they went into the cave or else wait until they had cut their way into the bank vault and try to catch them there. He could have somebody at the cave mouth to grab any who got away.

Whatever he did, he was determined to make them open the safes in Oyler's and Dibble's stores. In one of them would be the money stolen from the men coming to ransom relatives. Thinking of the men they had killed, Trego couldn't imagine a punishment bad enough for them.

Coy came back to town first. He came right to the parsonage. Trego took him down to the livery barn where he'd asked the others to meet him. Roger Sorenson had asked to join in when he heard what was planned.

A half hour before sundown, Pace Holcomb came in followed by Tom Ekhart in his wagon. His wife and daughter had come to spend the evening with Mrs. Bridgewood.

"We saw Fred Petrauk and Grumpy Rush heading for town as we came in," Tom Ekhart said.

"Good," Trego said. "We must be guessing right." He turned to Roger Sorenson. "Is this the night that Adalbert stays here at Genesis?"

Sorenson nodded. "He brought in the stage from Sage City today. He'll take the one back tomorrow."

"They're gathering like coyotes at a buffalo jump," Trego said. "Everything points to tonight. Roger, you and Pace watch from here. One of you can see the mouth of the cave from the far corner of the corral. Let us know if you see anybody go in there. Then get down there where you can smoke up anybody trying to get out. I'll take Tom and Oscar with me. We'll keep tabs on Oyler and Dibble."

Trego knew that he'd be the first target if it came to a battle. He'd given some of these men trouble ever since he came here and they hated him. He didn't worry about getting in their gun sights but rather that they would get away with the money. Trego had never had five thousand dollars of his own before, and he didn't propose letting thieves get away with it now.

Trego met Bridgewood at the corner of his house. He was pacing nervously back and forth, turning at every step to look at the bank.

"I locked everything," he said as if repeating it for the fiftieth time. "They can't break in."

"They won't go in the door," Trego said. "They'll go in through the cave."

He hadn't told Bridgewood about the trapdoor in the floor of Oyler's store. That might be the way they would go in. If so they'd surely come back out through the store. Trego intended to be watching.

Suddenly a scream came from Oyler's house behind the store. The door of Oyler's house flew open and Trego saw somebody come running from the house. It was too dark to identify the runner positively but he thought it was Alvena. He hurried over behind the drugstore to meet the runner.

"What's the matter?" Trego asked when he saw that it was Alvena.

She grabbed his arm. "It's Pa!" she sobbed. "He's awful sick. I think he's dying."

Trego turned to Ekhart. He saw Coy running back toward the livery barn. He'd relay this news to the men there.

"I'm going up there," Trego said. "Maybe I can do something."

"I'll come along," Ekhart said.

As soon as Trego stepped into the room and saw Cal Oyler on the bed moaning and clutching his stomach, he knew that Alvena hadn't been exaggerating.

"There's no doctor here," Neleda Oyler moaned, wringing her hands. "I don't know what's wrong so I can't doctor him."

Trego thought he knew. He stepped to the bed. "Can you hear me, Cal?" he said, bending over the man. "Where have you been?"

"Dibble's," Oyler moaned then groaned louder than ever.

"Did you drink anything there?"

Oyler nodded his head, but didn't try to speak. Trego stepped back to the other room where Cal's wife had retreated.

"Did Cal have a fight with Dibble?" he asked.

"They had a bad argument," Neleda said.

"What does that have to do with it?"

"Cal has been poisoned," Trego said. "Dibble tried to poison me with that special pitcher of lemonade yesterday. His dog drank it and died. Do you know where Dibble is now?"

"Home, I suppose," Alvena said. "What can we do?"

"I don't know," Trego said. "Do whatever you do for poison."

He hurried outside. He saw Petrauk and Rush among the people milling around outside. It was amazing how quickly a tragedy like this brought the curious. Sorenson, Pace, and Coy were there, too, having come up from the barn.

Cautiously, Trego went to Dibble's house, but it was dark and empty. When he came back, he saw that Petrauk and Rush were gone, too. It hit him then like the kick of a mule. They were striking at the bank while everyone was watching Cal Oyler die.

## 20

Trego found Ekhart and sent him to round up the others. Then he waited between the general store and the drugstore, planning his counterattack. As the men came running, he quickly assigned jobs. There were no questions. Trego was accepted as the leader.

"Tom, you and Mr. Bridgewood watch the bank. You'd better unlock the door and go inside where you can hear if they are really trying to get through the floor. Oscar, you stay here and keep the women calmed down. They'll be worried."

"If Mr. Bridgewood and Tom need help, I'll come and tell you," Coy said.

Trego nodded. "I'll take Pace and Roger with me. We'll go down to the cave. They obviously slipped down there while we were all up here. Likely they don't know we're on to what they're planning and they think this is the perfect opportunity to clean out the bank and disappear."

Trego led the way across the street, past the bank, and down the path behind it to the cave. It was dark inside the cave but far back, Trego could see some lights. Motioning for the other two to follow, he stepped inside. The floor was uneven but they didn't dare use a light. The torches up ahead were their only guide.

Trego moved cautiously. He could hear some pounding and sawing up ahead and hoped that would smother any noise they made. Suddenly he caught a movement only a short distance ahead, part way between his position and those torches. He reached a hand back and touched Pace who stopped Sorenson with the same movement. After watching and listening for a full minute, Trego saw the movement again. There was a man just ahead. He must have been left as a guard but likely he was more interested in what was going on under the bank than the chance that someone would find them.

"Stay here," he whispered to Pace. "I'll sneak up on him."

Lifting his gun, he moved silently forward, keeping his eye on the spot where he'd seen the man. When he moved again, Trego was close enough to distinguish his outline. He was a big man and, as Trego had hoped, he had his back to him, watching the progress of the men under the bank.

Trego let his eyes run ahead to those men. There were three of them. Their torches lit up the area as they worked on the floor above their heads. Trego brought his attention back to the man just ahead of him. He moved forward quietly then, swinging the gun, chopped the man along the side of the head. The man staggered and fell without making a sound.

Trego waited to make sure that the three men working by torchlight hadn't noticed. Hurrying back to Pace and Sorenson, he motioned them forward. The sawing up ahead had stopped. Trego saw that there were only two men in sight now and one of them was reaching up to the hole that had been sawed in the floor.

"Tie up this man with his own belt," Trego whispered to Sorenson. "When he comes to, take him up to the town hall and watch him."

"Who is it?" Pace asked.

"Grumpy Rush," Trego said. "So that has to be Petrauk and Dibble up ahead. But who is the third one?"

"Adalbert," Pace suggested.

Trego nodded. For the moment, he'd forgotten about the stage driver. With Oyler no longer a factor, the odds were favoring Trego and his men.

When the last man ahead had pulled himself up through the hole, Trego led Pace forward almost at a trot. There were two torches just below the hole where the men had left them. One torch was gone. That would be up in the vault.

Close to the torches, Trego stopped. There were splintered chunks of board and sawdust scattered around. They had apparently battered a hole in the floor, then sawed the jagged ends of the boards so they could pull themselves through without getting splinters. It gave Trego an idea. He moved forward, gathering the pieces of boards and raking up some sawdust. It was dry as only wood that has been protected from the elements for a long time can be.

He laid some rocks directly under the hole then stacked the pieces of boards on the rocks, adding the sawdust to the top of the pile. Seeing the oil can they had brought, apparently to keep the saw blade well lubricated, he squirted oil on the sticks. Then he jammed one of the lighted torches between the rocks under the pile.

The wood and sawdust ignited quickly and the oil sent up a dark cloud of smoke. With no air current in the cave, the smoke rose through the hole into the vault.

"Be ready," Trego whispered to Pace. Each man gripped his cocked revolver.

A yell came from above, then one man swung his legs through the hole. Trego fired a shot, nicking a leg. A startled yell echoed in the vault above and the legs disappeared.

There were wild shouts in the vault now and one man yelled that they'd get out above. Trego wondered if it was possible to get out of the vault from the inside.

While he was considering that, he heard someone running along the floor of the cave toward them. He turned his gun that way and waited for them to get close enough for the fire to light up their faces. He wasn't surprised to see Oscar Coy, but he was amazed to see Vona.

"What are you doing here?" he demanded.

"I came to tell you that the thieves are breaking into the bank," Coy said. "Mr. Bridgewood thinks he needs help up there. Vona just latched onto me and came, too."

"I can do something to help," Vona said. "All the money Pa has is in that bank."

Trego realized that Coy and Vona should be able to keep those men from coming down through the hole, especially while that fire was still burning. He might be needed up above. Maybe Bridgewood had his safe rigged so it could be unlocked from the inside.

"Keep those three in the vault," Trego said. He saw that Coy had a gun. He handed his to Vona. "Can you use this?"

She nodded. "If I have to. But you'll need it."

"I'll get Rush's gun as I go out. Just shoot at anything that comes down out of that vault."

"We can handle that, all right," Coy said.

Trego started on a run back toward the mouth of the cave. He was aware that Pace was following, but he had no worry about Coy and Vona being able to handle the situation below the bank. Once he got up to the bank, he'd have Bridgewood open the vault and they'd bring the robbers out that way.

Rush was on his feet but still addle-minded when Trego reached him and Sorenson. He grabbed the gun that Sorenson had taken from Rush, and he and Pace ran on.

Puffing as they reached the bank, they turned in. The outside door was open and Bridgewood and Ekhart were inside. Bridgewood was hopping around like a cat on a hot griddle.

"They're in there stealing all my money,"

he half screamed. "What can we do?"

"Open the vault," Trego said. "We'll have our guns on them when the door comes open."

Bridgewood gingerly moved to the door and started turning the big dial. Tom Ekhart and Pace stood to one side with guns in hand. Trego stood almost directly in front of the door. He'd get the first shot if bullets were needed.

"There was a shot down below just a couple of minutes ago," Ekhart said as Bridgewood worked. "Somebody must have tried to get away."

Trego frowned. He had been sure the robbers wouldn't try again to go through that hole after he had nicked that one in the leg.

The door swung open then, and Trego shoved his cocked gun forward. The interior of the vault was blue with oily smoke. Trego saw two men. Adalbert was standing with his hands high above his head. Petrauk was on the floor, leaning against the wall, holding his leg. Neither man had a gun in his hand.

Trego leaped into the vault, his gun still on the two. "Where's Dibble?"

"He went down that hole," Adalbert said.

"Used me as bait," Petrauk moaned. "Made me stick my legs down there. I got shot. Then he dropped through there so fast they didn't have time to shoot him."

"He's little enough he just jumped through," Adalbert added.

"Take care of these two," Trego said, and leaped over to the hole.

One torch was still burning down there but the oily wood was almost gone. He poked his head down and yelled. He didn't want Coy shooting at him. His yell was greeted by silence.

"You'd better not go down there," Pace said. "Coy would answer if he could."

Trego knew that Dibble might be waiting for him, but he couldn't take time to go back around. Vona was down there, too. He couldn't believe that Dibble would hurt her. But then he'd had a hard time believing that Dibble would poison people, too.

"I'm sick," Petrauk moaned. "Can you get me something?"

For just a moment, Trego's attention was pulled back to the vault. "You're just shot," he said.

"I'm awful sick," Petrauk repeated.

Trego's eyes swept the vault, lighted now by Bridgewood's lantern. There was paper money scattered over the floor. The torch the men had brought in was still burning, leaning in the corner against the vault's steel wall. There was a bottle near Petrauk.

"Where did you get that?" Trego asked.

"Dibble had it. We were celebrating getting in here." Petrauk groaned again. "That was before we knew anybody had found out."

"Did Dibble drink from that bottle, too?" Trego asked.

A deep frown pulled Petrauk's brow down as if he was having trouble concentrating. Adalbert answered.

"No. Fred got the first drink. I was to get the next one, but that's when that smoke started coming up through the hole and we forgot all about the bottle."

"You've been poisoned," Trego said to Petrauk. He looked at Adalbert. "You would have been next. Then Dibble would have had all the money for himself. He would have eliminated Grumpy the same way."

Petrauk still had enough presence of mind to swear groggily. Trego turned back to the hole cut in the floor. He was a big man but then Petrauk was a big man in girth, too, and the hole had been made big enough for him so Trego could make it.

Although he knew he might be shot the minute he descended through the hole, Trego dropped his feet down then slid through, his arms above his head. It would be like shooting a crippled dog to kill him. But no shot came.

Once he got his hands down, Trego made a fast turn, looking for Dibble. He wasn't there. Neither was Vona. Oscar Coy was sprawled on the floor of the cave, about where Trego had left him and Vona. He hurried over to him. He was alive but unconscious. Apparently Dibble had rapped him on the head and taken Vona with him. Why hadn't they shot him? Trego wondered.

Grabbing the torch, he circled the area, looking for the tracks of Dibble and Vona. He found them quickly, Vona's tracks pointing up the narrow tunnel toward Oyler's store, where she hadn't gone before.

Trego pieced it together rapidly. The money stolen from the victims coming to ransom their kidnapped relatives evidently was stored in Oyler's safe. Knowing the club Oyler held over Dibble, it was reasonable that Oyler would keep the stolen money. Dibble was going to get that now and run, using Vona as a guarantee against pursuit.

Leaving the torch, Trego started up the tunnel as fast as he could go, crawling the last ten yards. The trapdoor into Oyler's store was open. Apparently Dibble intended to come back this way rather than risk running through the crowd of people gathered at Oyler's house just behind the store. Trego thought of waiting for Dibble to come back, but decided against that. He was in such cramped quarters, he couldn't do much here. And maybe he was guessing wrong. Dibble might try to leave through the store.

Pushing his way up to the door, he raised his head enough to see around. Dibble had pulled a box around between the safe and the window so that the light from his torch wouldn't hit the window. He was crouched in front of the safe, working the dial. Trego couldn't see Vona anywhere.

Carefully, he put his hands on the floor beside the trapdoor and lifted himself through the hole. He was almost through, when Dibble suddenly wheeled from the safe, a gun centered on Trego. Trego's gun was in his hand, but his hand was on the floor lifting him through the hole.

"Leave the gun there and come on up," Dibble said softly. "No noise."

Trego had no choice. He knew Dibble wouldn't hesitate to kill him. He was close now to realizing his goal of escaping with all the money. He wasn't sure how much Dibble had taken from the bank.

Trego pulled himself up into the room. He saw that the safe was open. Dibble had a sack and, with his gun and one eye on

Trego, he scooped the piles of paper money into it.

"Where's Vona?" Trego demanded.

"Where you can't get to her," Dibble said. "She's my ticket out of here. Move away from that hole."

Trego moved close to the counter, stalling for time till he could locate Vona. "How did you get Oyler's safe open?"

"I watched him open it one day," Dibble said with a touch of pride. "I memorized the combination. Now you stay put."

Dibble backed toward the other side of the store. Trego guessed he was going after Vona, apparently where he had tied her. Dibble backed into a keg and shot a glance behind him to see how to get around it. Trego took that second to dive behind the counter. Dibble spun back, but he didn't shoot. A shot in the store would bring an investigation from the crowd at Oyler's house just behind the store. That was why Dibble hadn't shot him when he first showed up.

Trego crept back under the cascade of cloth from the bolt that was still lying where it had been the night before. He caught a glimpse of Vona being untied from a rack holding spades and shovels. He saw that her hands were tied behind her back and she had a gag over her mouth.

Dibble pushed Vona around the store while he looked for Trego. But he couldn't maneuver Vona into some places, and he evidently felt that time was running out for him. He stopped searching and pushed Vona to the trapdoor. There he made her step down into the hole and slide out of sight.

Trego crept to the end of the counter, keeping out of Dibble's sight. Dibble swept the store with his eyes and his gun again, then put his feet through the hole and lowered himself with his hands. In one hand he held his gun; in the other the sack of money.

When Dibble's head disappeared, still holding himself with his hands, Trego lunged out, catching the trapdoor and slamming it shut. The door caught the fingers of both of Dibble's hands.

Trego threw himself on the door, crushing the druggist's fingers. Dibble's screams roared from the tunnel below. Trego jerked the sack of money from his one hand and the gun from the other. Then, not lessening his weight on the door, he pulled over the same keg that had been there last night. It felt as if it were full of nails. He worked it over on top of the door. Then he stepped off, adding a heavy box to the weight of the keg. Dibble continued to scream under the floor.

Bridgewood came puffing in the front door followed by a couple of men from Oyler's who had heard the screaming.

"Petrauk is dying," Bridgewood reported. "What's the screaming here?"

Trego indicated the trapdoor. "Dibble. Got his hands caught in the money jar. Watch that he doesn't get loose." Trego ran toward the outside door. "I'll yell at you from below when to move the barrel so Dibble's hands will come free."

Trego ran to the bank. Ekhart was gone, but Pace was in the open vault. Trego headed for the hole in the floor.

"Petrauk is breathing his last," Pace reported.

"I'm after Dibble," Trego said, and squeezed through the hole with no further explanation.

Once in the cave, he turned toward the tunnel again. At the start of the rise in the floor, he found Vona scooting down with her hands still tied. Trego stopped long enough to untie her hands and take off her gag. Dibble wasn't going anywhere now unless Bridgewood let him escape into the store.

"Are you all right?" he asked.

Vona nodded. "I'm sorry we let you down. Oscar shot the man who put his legs through the hole then suddenly Mr. Dibble just dropped through that hole like a rock. He had a gun on us before we could even react. He hit Oscar over the head and tied me up and made me go with him."

"I figured all that," Trego said. "I think Coy is reviving. Pace is up in the vault. Why don't you and Coy climb up there with him? I'm going after Dibble."

He hurried up the steep tunnel, crawling as he approached the end. Dibble had stopped screaming, but he was whimpering like a sick baby.

"My hands!" he moaned. "Every finger is broken."

"I don't doubt it," Trego said. "I'm going to have them open that door. You'll have more than broken fingers if you try to get away."

"I can't do anything with broken hands," Dibble moaned.

Trego yelled for Bridgewood to move the barrel. There was scraping above then the door came open. Dibble slumped down in front of Trego.

"Lift him out of here," Trego yelled.

It was Tom Ekhart who reached down and helped lift Dibble up through the hole into the store. Trego crawled up after him.

"Looks like we've got the money and the thief," Ekhart said.

"That sackful came from Oyler's safe," Trego said. "Where's Adalbert?"

"I took him down to the hall," Ekhart said. "Sorenson is there watching him and Rush."

Pace, Vona, and Coy came from the bank. Pace reported that Petrauk was dead. Alvena came into the store just a minute later. Cal Oyler had succumbed to the poison in spite of all they could do.

"That's two murders you've got to answer for, Dibble," Tom Ekhart said.

"My fingers!" Dibble moaned. "Get somebody to fix my fingers."

"You can get a doc in Sage Creek at the jail," Trego said.

"You won't be needing fingers where you're going, anyway," Bridgewood added with no hint of compassion.

Alvena had gone to the safe. "I've never seen inside this before," she said. "Pa said this was his business." She pushed things around in the safe then picked up a paper at the back. After looking at it, she handed it to Trego. "Can you make sense of that?"

Trego took one look and nodded. "These were the shares each of the gang members were to get." His eye ran down the names. "Everyone is here. Dibble, Petrauk, Rush, Skeen, Furtak, Adalbert. Altogether they were to get only a little more than half. Cal apparently was taking the lion's share. Dibble, you were to get only ten percent. Did you know that?"

The back of the paper had the list of how much was taken in each robbery. Trego's eyes fastened on the seven-thousand-dollar entry. That would be what they took from Luther. He'd get his five thousand, and he'd take the other two thousand back to Ruth.

"What are you going to do with your money now that you've got it back?" Bridgewood asked. "My bank's still in business."

"You'd better fix that hole in your floor," Trego suggested.

Leaving Dibble in Ekhart's custody, he went outside. The fresh night air felt good after the close quarters in that tunnel under the store. He was aware of Vona coming up beside him.

"Will you be leaving now that you've got your money?" she asked.

"That depends," Trego said. "Let's walk down to the canyon rim."

He reached out his big hand and she snuggled her tiny one inside it. At the canyon, Trego stopped and looked down into the shadows cast by the rising moon.

"There are only two things that can keep me here," Trego said thoughtfully. "One is this canyon country. I like it."

She asked the leading question. "And the other?"

He wrapped his long arms around her. "You guess," he said softly. "Do I stay?"

"We can have a fine ranch south of Pa's place between Ash Creek Canyon and Spring Canyon," she said. "Does that answer your question?"

It did.

# ABOUT THE AUTHOR

**Wayne C. Lee** was born to pioneering homesteaders near Lamar, Nebraska. His parents were old when he was born and it was an unwritten law since the days of the frontier that it was expected that the youngest child would care for the parents in old age. Having grown up reading novels by Zane Grey and William MacLeod Raine, Lee wanted to write Western stories himself. His best teachers were his parents. They might not be able to remember what happened last week by the time Lee had reached his majority, but they shared with him their very clear memories of the pioneer days. In fact they talked so much about that period that it sometimes seemed to Lee he had lived through it himself. Lee wrote a short story and let his mother read it. She encouraged him to submit it to a magazine and said she would pay the postage. It was accepted and appeared as

*Death Waits at Paradise Pass* in *Lariat Story Magazine.* In the many Western novels that he has written since, violence has never been his primary focus, no matter what title a publisher might give one of his stories, but rather the interrelationships between the characters and within their communities. These are the dominant characteristics in all of Lee's Western fiction and create the ambiance so memorable in such diverse narratives as *The Gun Tamer* (1963), *Petticoat Wagon Train* (1972), and *Arikaree War Cry* (1992). In the truest sense Wayne C. Lee's Western fiction is an outgrowth of his impulse to create imaginary social fabrics on the frontier and his stories are intended primarily to entertain a reader at the same time as to articulate what it was about these pioneering men and women that makes them so unique and intriguing to later generations. His pacing, graceful style, natural sense of humor, and the genuine liking he feels toward the majority of his characters, combined with a commitment to the reality and power of romance between men and women as a decisive factor in making it possible for them to have a better life together than they could ever hope to have apart, are what most distinguish his contributions to the Western story.

We hope you have enjoyed this Large Print book. Other Thorndike, Wheeler, Kennebec, and Chivers Press Large Print books are available at your library or directly from the publishers.

For information about current and upcoming titles, please call or write, without obligation, to:

Publisher
Thorndike Press
295 Kennedy Memorial Drive
Waterville, ME 04901
Tel. (800) 223-1244

or visit our Web site at:

http://gale.cengage.com/thorndike

OR

Chivers Large Print
published by BBC Audiobooks Ltd
St James House, The Square
Lower Bristol Road
Bath BA2 3SB
England
Tel. +44(0) 800 136919
email: bbcaudiobooks@bbc.co.uk
www.bbcaudiobooks.co.uk

All our Large Print titles are designed for easy reading, and all our books are made to last.